South to Sonora

After a ten-year prison term for killing a man he'd found molesting a girl, all Tom Jericho wants is a quiet life. But the State Governor offers him a deal: the notorious Crane Gang are planning something big, and the governor wants to know what it is. Jericho had befriended the youngest of the Crane boys in the pen and, with Lee now being transported across the desert, all Jericho has to do is help him escape, infiltrate the gang and uncover the plan.

Before he knows it, Jericho is in Mexico, the revolution raging all around him. One false move could mean a dusty grave in the hot, dry earth of Sonora. . . .

South to Sonora

Michael Stewart

A Black Horse Western

ROBERT HALE · LONDON

Robert Hale Limited
Clerkenwell House
Clerkenwell Green
London EC1R 0HT

www.halebooks.com

Typeset by
Derek Doyle & Associates, Shaw Heath
Printed and bound in Great Britain by
CPI Antony Rowe, Chippenham and Eastbourne

Dedicated to Betty Stewart, without whom nothing would have been possible.

CHAPTER ONE

When Tom Jericho was released from state prison he only returned to his home town so that he could pay his respects at his parents' graves, otherwise he wouldn't have gone.

His plan was, get off the train, go to the cemetery, say a prayer or two, then get back on the train and never come back.

The trouble with that plan was that his home town, Endurance, was the place where he'd killed the man. Not deliberately, otherwise Jericho would've been hanged long ago, but that wouldn't wash much with the dead man's brothers. And there was only one train a day passed through Endurance, which meant he'd have to spend a whole day and night there. So, all things considered, Jericho figured that visiting his parents' graves was going to be something of a risky business.

He hadn't even got off the train before the word had gone out that he was coming.

Jericho couldn't get a train directly to his home town. He'd had to change trains at Personville, and that's where Bob Larson saw him. And straight away, Larson scuttled off to the telegraph office and wired the Robbins boys that the man who'd beaten their brother to death with his bare hands was coming to town.

Jericho's train took three hours to travel from Personville to Endurance. That was enough time for the telegraph operator to write down the message and have someone ride over to the Robbins place with it. But the Robbins place was a ranch, and pretty spread out, which meant that by the time Jericho arrived in Endurance, not all the boys had been gathered together in the ranch house and told the news.

Jericho stepped down off the train, dressed in the same clothes he'd been wearing when he was sent to prison ten years earlier. They were looser now, and he had to wear his belt tighter by a couple of notches. He'd lost a little fat over the past decade, and some muscle too. And he was bearded now.

Hell, he thought. Probably nobody'll recognize me at all. I'll be just anoher stranger, passing through.

Whether or not he'd changed, the town certainly had. Endurance was a proper city now, almost as big as Tucson.

Even the depot building had changed. The old wooden structure had been replaced by a larger brick one. And Spence, the old guy who'd run the station single-handed, had been replaced too. Probably dead, Jericho figured. Spence had already been older than Methuselah's grandpappy when Jericho was a boy.

Jericho passed through the depot building and out the other side, back into the glaring Arizona sunlight.

What had been the only street in Endurance was now called Main Street. Jericho knew this because a sign high up on the corner of a building said so. Before he'd beaten Virgil Robbins to death, before he'd been sent away to State Prison, Jericho could have walked down the middle of this street safely enough, but he couldn't now. Not without getting trodden into the earth by any one of the multitude of horses and wagons that were making their way up and down it. He stuck to the boardwalk.

Eventually he reached the end of the street, and had left the town behind and was climbing the dusty trail uphill to the cemetery.

The town had expanded, and so had the graveyard. It had spread down the slope furthest from the town, so the oldest part, on the crown of the hill, was the part he reached first. He hunted around, reading the tombstones and markers, but couldn't find any mention of his folks' names.

'You'll be looking a long time, Jericho,' shouted a voice from behind him.

Jericho didn't turn round. He had a feeling he

recognized the voice, though he couldn't be sure. It sounded like Elmer, eldest of the three Robbins boys. Virgil Robbins, the youngest, was the one Jericho had killed.

'Your ma and pa ain't here,' jeered the voice.

Only now did Jericho turn. Sure enough, the owner of the voice was Elmer Robbins, who'd been thin, twenty-and-some and butt ugly when Jericho had last seen him. Now he was fat, thirty-and-some and even uglier, if that was possible. He had a man on either side of him. The younger one to the left would, Jericho guessed, be Cal, the middle brother. And the fella to the right of Elmer was Old Man Robbins himself: old and gnarled and mean, kept alive by liquor and spite.

'They're supposed to be buried here,' Jericho said, keeping his voice level. 'They arranged for two plots, side by side, for when they died. Paid for them, and all. So how come they ain't here?'

Elmer hawked and spat, decorating a tombstone with yellow phlegm. 'See, the thing is,' he said, 'after you were sent to prison for killing Virgil, the good people of Endurance figured they didn't want the kin of no murderer buried where decent people are laid to rest. . . .'

Jericho kept his breathing low and even. 'So where are they buried?'

Elmer shrugged. 'Out in the desert somewhere. I don't rightly recollect.' He grinned.

'Who buried 'em?'

Elmer took off his hat and scratched his head. 'It's all so long ago, I don't recall that either.' He put his hat back on his head and hooked his thumb around his gunbelt, close to where his six-gun hung at his hip.

The sun beat down. After all his years cooped-up in prison, Jericho wasn't used to the heat. He could feel it sapping his energy, and his head began to spin, but he was damned if he was going to show weakness in front of the Robbins clan. 'I ain't no murderer,' said Jericho.

Old Man Robbins opened his toothless mouth and screamed, 'You murdered my boy!'

Jericho said, 'It was a fair fight.'

The other brother, Cal, must've figured it was high time he said something. 'Weren't no fair fight: you were twice his size.'

'And he was twice the size of the girl he'd dragged into that barn,' said Jericho.

'Becky Parsons was a whore,' yelled the old man. 'She wanted it!'

'Becky Parsons was little more than a child,' said Jericho.

'Don't matter none now,' said Elmer. 'Fact is, you killed Virgil, and now we're gonna kill you. I figure a minute or so from now, you're going to be saying "Hi", to your ma and pa in person.'

'I ain't carrying a gun,' said Jericho.

Elmer laughed. 'Where you're going, you won't need one!'

11

Most of the grave markers weren't stone, but wood. Jericho thought: even if he dodged behind one of them, they wouldn't offer any kind of protection worth a damn. Further down the hill, in the newer part of the cemetery, there were a few headstones, even a tomb with a weeping angel – in marble or some such – perched on top of it. But even if he could take cover behind the tomb, so what? It was still one unarmed man against three men with guns. Whichever way he played it, Jericho figured he was going to end up dead.

At least he could take one of them with him.

Maybe.

'It's getting kind of hot up here,' Elmer said. 'If it's all the same to you, I think maybe we'll get this done, then go into town, find a nice cool saloon, have ourselves a drink, Shame you won't be joining us, Jericho. . . .' He drew his gun and levelled it at Jericho's chest.

'Everybody will know you murdered me,' Jericho told him. 'You'll hang.'

Elmer shook his head. 'By the time anybody else gets up here, you'll have a gun in your hand. Show him, Cal.'

Cal reached into his jacket and pulled out an old .31 calibre 5-shot pocket revolver. 'We brought this along, just in case you weren't wearing no gun,' Cal said.

'Looks like you thought of everything,' said Jericho.

12

'Enough of this jawing,' yelled the old man. 'I've waited all these years for revenge, and I don't wanna wait a minute longer!' His shaking, claw-like hand reached for his gun.

There was about twenty feet between Jericho and Elmer. When he was a kid, Jericho could have hit a playing card at that distance, but thanks to his years in prison, he was out of practice. Not carrying a gun had never bothered him much, but Jericho always felt kind of incomplete without a throwing knife on him. So he'd bought one in Personville, while he'd been waiting for the train to Endurance, meaning to start practising again as soon as he got the chance.

It looked like he wasn't going to get any practising done after all.

Jericho reached behind him, slipped the knife free of the sheath fastened to his belt, and in one fluid motion sent it spinning through the dry Arizona air. He hit the dirt the same moment the blade of the knife buried itself hilt-deep in Elmer's forehead. Elmer's body went into spasm, his finger jerking at the trigger, and Jericho felt the rush of air as the .45 bullet zinged over his head.

'Elmer!' yelled the old man, pulling his gun clear of its holster.

The other brother, Cal, was already levelling his gun at Jericho, and all Jericho could do was stare at the black eye of the barrel.

A second gunshot rang through the desert air.

CHAPTER TWO

Jericho wondered why he wasn't dead. He opened his eyes and saw Cal, still standing there, still pointing his gun. But the life had gone from his eyes. Cal's knees buckled and he crumpled forward into the dirt, and it was only then, when his Stetson rolled away, that Jericho saw that the back of Cal's head was missing.

Old Man Robbins spun around and saw his other boy was now dead, too. He gave a wordless animal cry, dropped his pistol and rushed to where Cal lay.

Jericho pushed himself up off the ground, and it was only then that he saw the half-dozen men riding up the hill from town. Sunlight glinted off the badges pinned to the men's vests.

Lawmen.

Jericho knew better than to make any sudden movements. He stood still as a statue as the men rode up the track to the cemetery. The lead man, older than the others, had to be the sheriff, Jericho guessed. The man immediately behind him, still with his Winchester rifle in his hand, was the one who'd shot Cal.

The old man was crying bitterly, his whole body shaking as he sobbed, cradling first the body of his son Cal, then his other boy, Elmer. 'All my boys dead!' he wailed. 'All my boys dead!'

Jericho couldn't help feeling sorry for him. He knew that the old man had been mean and twisted-up for as long as anyone could remember – that he'd raised his sons to be the same, and was therefore partly responsible for their deaths.

But even so. . . .

The lawmen reached the top of the hill. The sheriff said, 'You Tom Jericho?'

'Yeah.'

'You're coming with me.'

'Why?' said Jericho. 'I ain't done nothing but defend myself.'

The grey-haired sheriff eyed Jericho. He didn't look like a man who was in the mood for arguing. 'I don't much care about what you done, or what you ain't. You're coming with me, and that's all there is to it.'

Jericho figured if that's the way the sheriff wanted it, that's how it had to be.

But in the meantime, if Old Man Robbins had his way, Jericho wasn't going anywhere. His sobbing had turned back into anger, and the lion's share of that anger was directed at Jericho.

The old man scrabbled over to where he'd

dropped his gun, plucked it off the ground and screamed, 'My boys are dead because of you, you son of a bitch!' He fired, the retort sounding more like a shotgun than a revolver.

Next to Jericho, a wooden grave marker exploded in a shower of splinters. Fury had ruined the old man's aim. Before he could fire another shot, one of the sheriff's deputies had ridden up behind him and pistol whipped him.

Old Man Robbins's eyes glazed over and he fell unconscious to the ground.

'Think we better find him a cell, boys,' said the sheriff. Then he turned to Jericho. 'You were just released from state prison, right?'

'That's right,' said Jericho.

The sheriff pulled out his tobacco pouch and rolled himself a cigarette as he watched a couple of his deputies haul the unconscious Robbins across the back of a horse. 'All of you fellas head down to the jailhouse. Me and Mr Jericho here will follow you down. Matt, you better tell the undertaker he's got a couple of new clients up here.'

The man called Matt – the one who'd done the fancy shooting with the Winchester – nodded, and the deputies started making their way back down the hill to town.

The sheriff lit his cigarette and breathed smoke, watching his men till they were out of earshot. Then he turned back to Tom Jericho and said, 'You big friends of the state governor or something?'

16

Jericho raised an eyebrow. 'Me? Now what makes you think a high-and-mighty gentleman like the state governor would want to be friends with me? That idea is just plum loco, Sheriff.'

'That's what I figure,' said the sheriff. 'So tell me why I got a letter from the governor's office, hand-delivered to me less than an hour ago, telling me to make sure that Thomas Juan Antonio Jericho gets back safely on that train tomorrow? You don't suppose there were two Thomas Juan Antonio Jerichos on that train you came in on?'

Jericho scratched his chin. 'I figure that'd be a mite unlikely,' he said. 'And I kind of wish they hadn't sent that letter, Sheriff.'

'Good thing for you they did,' he told him. 'That letter arrived on the same train as you. As things were, I got here only just in time to save your hide.'

That was true. Jericho tipped his hat. 'And much obliged I surely am,' he said.

The sheriff said, 'The governor could've sent the message by telegraph. It would've got to me. I can only figure one reason why he wrote a sealed letter instead.'

'And why's that?'

'Because he wanted the message to be a secret, and too many people get to read a telegraph before it reaches the person it's meant for.'

Jericho didn't say anything to that.

He peered at Jericho speculatively. 'You know, I got a suspicion there's more to you than meets the eye.'

17

Jericho smiled. 'I'd appreciate it if you kept that particular suspicion to yourself,' he said.

Thirty minutes or so later, in the jailhouse, the sheriff showed Jericho the letter that had been sent from the governor's office. In fancy language it told the sheriff that if Tom Jericho was so stupid as to spend a day in his old home town of Endurance, then the stay had better be a peaceable one, otherwise the governor would have the sheriff's badge.

'I have a dozen questions I could ask you,' said the sheriff, 'but I somehow get the feeling I wouldn't get no answers.'

Jericho put the letter down on the desk. 'You're right there,' he said. He looked around him. There wasn't anybody else in the immediate vicinity. 'Anyone else know what it says in that letter?'

'Nope,' said the sheriff. 'Only me.'

'Not even your deputies?'

'Not even them. They just do what I tell 'em.'

'I'd appreciate it if you let it stay that way,' said Jericho.

The sheriff picked up the letter, folded it a couple of times and pushed it into his vest pocket. 'Figured you might,' he said. 'And *I'd* appreciate it if you'd accept my offer of a room for the night.'

'You mean one of those *rooms* you got with the bars?' Jericho rolled himself a cigarette.

The sheriff smiled. 'This may not be the swankiest hotel in town,' he said, 'but it's sure the safest. We'll

18

let you keep the door unlocked, though – on account of you being an honoured guest.'

Jericho struck a match and held it to the end of his cigarette. He drew in the rich smoke and said, 'Since you've invited me so nicely, sheriff, I don't see how I can refuse.'

The sheriff pulled open a desk drawer and pulled out a couple of glasses. He set them on the desktop side by side, reached back down into the drawer and this time pulled out a bottle of whiskey. He poured the booze and pushed one of the glasses towards Jericho. He proposed a toast. 'To a peaceful night's sleep,' he said.

Jericho picked up the glass. 'I'll second that,' he said, and drank the whiskey slowly, rolling it around his mouth before letting it slip down his throat.

Now that they'd drunk their toast, the sheriff opened another desk drawer, and this time brought out a gun in a holster. He placed it on the desk between them. 'You recognize this?'

Jericho nodded. 'That's Old Man Robbins's gun. The one he was gonna kill me with a little while back in the cemetery.'

The sheriff pulled the gun from the holster. 'You see anything unusual about it?'

Jericho shrugged. 'Looks like any other six-gun.'

'It ain't no six-gun.'

'It ain't?'

'Nope.' He broke the gun open. 'It takes nine cartridges, not six. And those cartridges don't have to be

19

regular bullets. They can be full of pellets – like a shotgun cartridge, only smaller. They made thousands of these guns years ago. They were very popular with officers in the Confederate cavalry.'

'That a fact?' said Jericho, wondering where this was going.

'You know that Old Man Robbins was a Confederacy cavalry officer?'

'I think maybe somebody told me that once, yeah. When I was a kid.'

'Now you've had a good look at this revolver,' said the sheriff, pouring them each another glass of whiskey, 'you think you might have seen others like it?'

Jericho said, 'I guess. Not often, but yeah – I've seen guns like it.'

'Me too,' said the sheriff. He scratched his chin. 'You know I've been sheriff here for seven years?'

'Yeah?'

'So I'd been here a year when your folks died.'

Jericho felt his blood freeze. He'd known the man was leading up to something, but hadn't guessed it had anything to do with his ma and pa. 'Whatever you're trying to tell me, Sheriff, I sure wish you'd get to it sooner.'

The sheriff eyed Jericho steadily. 'Your ma and pa were shot with a gun like this one,' he said.

CHAPTER THREE

'That ain't true,' said Jericho, his voice rising. 'There was a fire. An accident. Goddamn oil lamp or something. They died in their sleep!'

'I saw their bodies,' the sheriff told him. 'They'd both been shot in the head, but not with no ordinary bullets. They'd been shot with cartridges filled with pellets. Their wounds were like shotgun blasts, only smaller. . . ' He touched the old Confederate cavalry revolver lying on the table. 'The kind of wounds that a gun like this would make. . . .'

Jericho stood up suddenly, the chair he'd been sitting on crashing backwards on to the stone floor. 'You telling me that Old Man Robbins killed my ma and pa?' He reached for the pistol on the table, intending to go to the back of the jailhouse, where the old man was in a cell, still out cold, and kill him with his own damn gun. But before he could grab the pistol, the sheriff's fist lashed out and connected with Jericho's chin.

The next thing Jericho knew, he was lying on the floor next to the chair he'd toppled over, groggy and with an aching jaw.

As the mists cleared he gingerly probed his mouth with his fingers and was relieved to find he had the same number of teeth he'd had before he'd been punched.

'That's a mean right hand you've got there, Sheriff,' he said.

The sheriff was now using that same right hand to point his gun at Jericho. 'You just stay down there while I finish what I'm telling you. I ain't forgot about that letter from the governor telling me to take good care of you, but if I have to pistol-whip you like I did the old man, I will. Understand?'

'I understand,' said Jericho. 'But what I don't understand is why you didn't arrest Robbins if you knew he'd killed my folks.'

The sheriff walked slowly around the table and perched himself on the edge of it, all the time taking care to keep his gun pointed at his guest. 'Remember me saying how there were thousands of them nine-shot pistols made? You said yourself, you've seen guns like it before. Not often maybe, but you've seen 'em. Which means that although Robbins is the only man I've ever seen around here with one, it don't mean there ain't more.'

Jericho swore. 'That's enough proof for me,' he said. 'Most towns, they've hanged men without any proof at all.'

'Not any town I've been sheriff of.'

'Well,' said Jericho, 'ain't that just my luck? Here in Endurance we must have just about the only sheriff west of the Mississippi who abides by the law!'

'You reckon?'

'I reckon.'

'And what was the name of the sheriff who was here when you killed Virgil Robbins?'

Tom Jericho had to think for a moment, it had been so long. 'Quaid,' he said at last. 'Ed Quaid.'

The sheriff nodded. 'Good man from what I heard. I also heard that if it weren't for him, Old Man Robbins and his other boys would have lynched you from the nearest tree. Instead, Sheriff Quaid saved your hide so you could get judged fair and square in a courtroom.'

So far as Jericho was concerned, the judge should have given him a damn medal for killing Virgil Robbins, not sent him to state prison, not after what had been done to Becky Parsons. Jericho hadn't killed him deliberately; he'd been angry and let loose with his fists, knocking Virgil down, and Virgil had hit his head on an iron spike somebody had driven into the ground to throw horseshoes at.

Ten years or so later, lying on the floor of the sheriff's office, the ache in his jaw easing some, Jericho nodded. 'I get your point. Sheriff Ed Quaid upheld the law. If it weren't for him, I'd be dead and forgotten. What happened to him, anyway?'

'Shot in the back,' said the sheriff. 'No good

reason. Just some drunk who couldn't even remember he'd done it when he woke up the next morning. After that, I got the job.'

'The drunk hang?'

'Yeah.'

'What happened to Becky Parsons?'

'The girl Virgil Robbins molested?'

'Yeah – though molested don't really cover what he did.'

'She and her folks left town. Crying shame. Nice people.'

'Yeah.' Jericho shifted uncomfortably on the floor. 'You planning on letting me up anytime soon?'

'Maybe,' replied the sheriff. 'It depends on whether you still want to do harm to Old Man Robbins. The way I see it, that man's gonna spend the rest of his life – which can't be very long – in misery now that all his sons are dead. And what'll make it worse is the knowledge, no matter what he tries to tell himself, that what happened to them is a result of him raising them to be as mean-spirited as he is. If you killed him now, it'd be a kindness. . . . Are you listening to any of this, or am I wasting my breath?'

'I hear you,' said Jericho. 'And, much as I'd like to shoot the evil son of a bitch, I think you have a point.'

The sheriff nodded. 'I heard a lot about you these last few years. Seems you were a man of your word. That still so?'

'I try my best.'

'Do I have your word you won't do Old Man Robbins any harm if I let you up?'

Jericho sighed. 'I give you my word, Sheriff.'

The sheriff slid his gun back into its holster. 'OK. You can get up.'

So Jericho got up, and spent the night sleeping on a bunk in one of the cells. It wasn't comfortable exactly, but at least it was a mite better than lying on the damn floor.

Back on the train the next afternoon, Jericho thought back to the downright peculiar thing that had happened only a few days earlier.

The day before he was due to be released, he'd been called to the warden's office. Jericho figured it was for some kind of 'I hope you've learned your lesson' speech, but when he'd got there, the guards who had escorted him were both dismissed – about which they didn't look too happy – and he was left alone with the warden and a grey-haired, distin-guished kind of a gentleman whom Jericho wasn't introduced to. Not at first, anyway.

'I understand you've served your country?' asked the warden.

Which was a question Jericho hadn't been expect-ing. He guessed the warden was referring to when he'd served in the army for a spell, back when he'd been just a pup. So Jericho said, 'Yes sir, Mr Warden, I was in the army.'

'I heard you earned yourself a medal for bravery?'

Jericho told him that was true. So the warden looked at the grey-haired gentleman, and the grey-haired gent looked at the warden, and the warden looked back at Jericho and said, 'You used to be friends with Lee Crane, am I correct?'

It took a moment for Jericho to recall who Lee Crane was. Then he got it. A nervy, small-boned youngster with a pointy face. This had been back in the early days of his incarceration. Jericho had seen Crane being picked on by a prisoner three times his size and without knowing anything about either man, just not liking what he saw, Jericho had clipped the bigger man on the chin, knocking him cold. And Lee had instantly become his friend for life. Turned out he was the younger brother of the notorious outlaw Walt Crane. The friendship hadn't lasted long, though. Lee, imprisoned for a minor crime, had been released a couple of years later, while Tom Jericho still had most of his sentence remaining. So Jericho looked at the warden and replied, 'Yes sir, I used to be friends with Lee Crane.'

To which the warden had said, 'Real good friends? Or just acquaintances, as you might say?'

Jericho hadn't seen any reason to lie. He shrugged. 'I don't suppose we'd have been friends if we'd met on the outside. But in prison, you ain't so choosy.'

The warder and the gent exchanged looks again, and the gent got up. Speaking for the first time since

Jericho had entered the room, he said, 'Do you love your country?'

Tom figured he loved his country about as much as anyone could after their country had locked them away for ten years, but this didn't seem the right time to say that. So he said, 'Yes, sir.' Which wasn't a lie exactly, it was just about true enough, on balance.

The grey-haired gentleman had a smooth voice, like treacle running off a spoon, and Jericho had a notion that he might be a politician of some kind. 'I'd like to offer you an opportunity to do your country a service, *and* make yourself some money,' he said.

'How much money?'

He replied, 'What were you thinking of doing, once you were free? You must have some dreams.'

Jericho thought for a moment. 'I had an idea I'd work, save money – enough to buy a farm. Maybe get a place up North California way. I been up there, once. Nice land.'

The grey-haired gentleman nodded. 'Very well. Enough money to buy a farm.'

So Tom Jericho found himself making a deal.

And that was how, only a few days later, he was on a train bound for Krugerville, with instructions to have himself charged with murder.

27

CHAPTER FOUR

When Tom Jericho got to Krugerville he checked into the Silver Lode Hotel and was given a room on one of the lower floors, at the back. Within two minutes of his arrival, there was a knock on his door. He opened it. Without a word, three men entered, two of them carrying a packing case. Once the door had been closed, the two men set down the case and opened it.

There was a dead body inside. It wasn't anybody Jericho knew.

The two men who'd been carrying the packing case now lifted out the body and placed it on the floor. Then the other man opened the door a little, checked no one was coming down the hall, and the other two left.

So now there was only this third man, and Jericho, and the corpse.

The man grinned and said, 'Nice to meet you. I'm Dan Harbin. Here – you'd better take this. . . .' He reached into his coat and pulled out a gun. Passing it to Jericho, he said, 'It would be kind of difficult to convince people you've shot somebody if you haven't got a gun.' Harbin reached into his coat again, this time producing a deck of cards. 'I suggest we wait an hour or so – say, till about six o'clock. I figure there should be a lot of witnesses around by then.'

They played a few hands of poker and blackjack, all the time Jericho trying not to be too distracted by the fact there was a corpse on the floor of his hotel room.

Eventually, Jericho said, 'Who was he, anyway?'

Harbin said, 'A vagrant. Died in a hospital bed last night. The booze killed him, so I'm told. Of course, once you've plugged him, nobody's gonna think he died any other way.'

'He looks like he's sleeping.'

'We got a professional embalmer to put some powder and rouge on him, so he looks fresh.'

'What about the blood?' asked Jericho.

Harbin's brow creased. 'What blood?'

'When he's shot, there won't be much blood. Won't people know he must have already been dead when he was shot?'

Harbin grinned. 'Nobody will look that close, believe me. They'll hear an argument, and the shot; see the body with a hole in it. . . . They'll all swear you killed him, don't worry about that.'

'That's reassuring,' said Jericho. 'One other thing.'

'What?'

'Would you mind shooting him?'

'But he's already dead.'

'I know,' said Jericho. 'But it just don't feel right, shooting a dead body.'

Harbin scratched his chin. 'OK. I don't mind.'

'Thanks,' said Jericho. 'You heard anything more about what Walt Crane and his gang are planning?'

'Nope,' said Harbin. 'And I want you to know, we all appreciate you helping us out this way. Just remember, once you're in the gang, keep your eyes and ears open, and leave them messages the way you've been shown.'

'*If* I get to be part of the gang,' said Jericho.

Hardin dealt another blackjack hand. 'Of course you will be. We've all got complete faith in you.'

'That's nice,' said Jericho.

A while later, Harbin pulled his pocket watch from his vest, squinted at it and said, 'It's about time. I figure about now, all the hotel guests will be resting or eating, or sprucing themselves up for the evening.'

'Shame we have to disturb them,' said Jericho.

'You ready?'

'I'm ready.'

Harbin leapt to his feet, scattering the deck of cards on to the bed. 'You cheating son of a bitch!' he yelled.

'Nobody calls me a cheating son of a bitch!'

shouted Jericho, at the top of his voice.

'I'm gonna pound you into the dirt!' yelled back Harbin. 'I'll break every bone on your body with my bare hands!'

'You get away from me, you varmint!' shouted Jericho.

Harbin pointed the gun at the corpse and fired twice into the chest. He handed the smoking six-gun to Jericho. 'Good luck!' he whispered.

'Thanks.'

Harbin climbed out of the window and jumped down into the alleyway behind the hotel. Jericho dropped the gun on to the bed along with the scattered playing cards, then he opened the carpet bag he'd arrived with and pulled out a bottle of whiskey.

Outside the room he could hear raised voices, men's and women's, saying:

'You hear that?'

'That was gunfire!'

'Where'd it come from?'

'That room. . . .'

'Across the hall. . . .'

And then doors opening; running feet.

Figuring it was going to be some little time before he was going to get another drink, he managed to swallow a good part of the whiskey before the first arrival burst in through the door.

He was a big man with a big moustache and a big revolver clutched in a big fist. Eyes widening, he looked at the corpse lying on the floor, then at

31

Jericho, then back at the corpse again.

Next into the room was a smaller man, also carrying a gun. He ran through the door so fast he almost collided with the larger man. Adam's apple bobbing, the smaller man said, 'What's going on here?'

There were other people out in the corridor. Once a couple of seconds had gone by and they realized there wasn't likely to be any more shooting, they all crowded around the doorway, trying to peek inside.

'Somebody better fetch the sheriff,' announced Jericho. 'I'm damned if I ain't just shot an unarmed man to death!'

Jericho couldn't help feeling that his arrest and confinement and trial were all very civilized. Not once did anybody suggest lynching him, which was a relief.

He was tried fair and square, with a judge and jury and everything, and sentenced to hang at the state penitentiary.

And so, two days later, he found himself being bundled into a specially armoured railway carriage, prior to being transported back to the same prison he'd been released from only the previous week.

There was only one other prisoner in the carriage – also on his way to the state penitentiary for an appointment with the hangman.

Lee Crane hadn't changed much in the eight years since Tom Jericho had last set eyes on him. He was still scrawny and nervous, and still seemed kind of young, despite his hair having thinned out some.

And Tom Jericho couldn't have changed as much as he thought he might have, because as soon as he climbed up into the carriage, his wrists and ankles shackled, Lee Crane looked at him, grinned, and said, 'Well, I'll be damned! If it ain't my old friend Tom Jericho!'

And Jericho grinned back and said, 'My, my. Small world, ain't it?'

The train had been thundering across the desert for an hour before the first explosion tore up the rails directly in front of it and sent the locomotive ploughing through the dirt. It was only by sheer luck that it didn't tip over on to its side.

Almost before the train had completely stopped, bullets began hitting both sides of the armoured carriage. The guards inside the carriage returned fire through the metal grilles that covered the windows, but that didn't stop the attack.

There were more explosions on either side of the carriage. They must have been smoke bombs of some kind, because suddenly there was thick yellow fog seeping in through the grilles, and everybody started to choke.

For the hundredth time since he'd first been called into the prison governor's office, Tom Jericho wondered what he'd signed himself up to. *How the hell was he supposed to help the Government of the United States of America stop some kind of massacre if he was going to be choked to death on this train?*

He heard one guard splutter, 'We gotta get the damn door open! We gotta get out of here!'

Another guard said, 'But they'll shoot us, soon as we get out there!'

'We got no choice! We stay in here, we're gonna die anyway!'

Jericho couldn't see anything now except for the thick yellow smoke swirling around him. It smelt foul. The smoke crawled up his nose and seeped into his mouth, forcing its stench into his lungs. It stung his eyes. He squeezed them shut, but that didn't help. Tears streamed down his cheeks.

Jericho heard the door being unlocked and swung open, and then there was a blast of sweet desert air. He heard the guards jumping out of the carriage; heard their feet hitting the dirt as they landed; heard them shout, 'Don't shoot! We surrender! Don't shoot!'

Then he heard the gunshots and the screams, and somebody yell, 'Kill 'em, boys!'

Then silence.

He would have escaped the carriage himself if he could, but he and Lee Crane were both chained. They sat side by side on a bench seat, their leg shackles threaded through iron hoops fixed to the floor.

So far they'd been forbidden to talk, but now Lee said, 'It's my brother! My brother's come to rescue me!'

To which Tom Jericho replied, 'Sorry to contradict you, Lee, but I think I just recognized a voice of an old friend of mine.'

'Whoever they are,' Lee said, 'I'm mighty grateful to 'em. They've saved me from the hangman!'

The smoke was clearing. Jericho wiped his sleeve across his eyes and saw a tall, rangy man enter through the open door of the carriage. It was Dan Harbin, whom Jericho had last seen climbing out of the window of his hotel room in Krugerville after pumping a couple of bullets into a vagrant's corpse. He was carrying a set of keys that he'd taken off one of the guards. 'Come on, Tom,' he said, 'let's go!'

'Hey – what about me?' yelled Lee Crane.

Dan grabbed Jericho and tried dragging him out of the carriage. 'We ain't got time to waste!'

Jericho resisted. 'I ain't going without Lee,' he said.

'What?'

'I said, I ain't going without Lee,' Jericho said. 'He's an old friend of mine from prison.'

Dan sighed. 'Aw hell, Tom – if you say so.' He went over to where Lee Crane was sitting, and unlocked the shackles from around his wrists and ankles. 'We only brought one extra horse,' Dan told Jericho.

'He can ride with me,' said Jericho.

Dan shrugged and jumped out of the carriage. Jericho turned to Lee. 'You OK?'

'Hell, yes!' said Lee, as they jumped down on to the desert sand.

There were five horsemen and one spare horse. Jericho climbed up into the saddle and hauled Lee up behind him. Dan gave a yell and set off towards the hills that rose on the south-west horizon. As they followed, Lee said to Jericho, 'I ain't never gonna forget this, Tom. Not as long as I live.'

Just then, one of the horsemen who'd helped the two condemned men escape saw something in the distance behind them. He shouted a warning to Dan Harbin and, when he slowed up, they all turned to see what was wrong.

There was a cloud of dust rising out of the desert about two miles behind them. Dan Harbin retrieved a telescope from out of his saddle-bag and squinted through it. 'There's a posse after us,' he said at last. 'About twenty men, I figure.'

He looked worried.

This wasn't part of the plan at all.

CHAPTER FIVE

As they rode for the distant hills, Tom Jericho tried to figure out what could have gone wrong. Maybe somebody had seen Dan Harbin and his men preparing to ambush the train – maybe when they'd obtained the explosives, or the gas bombs? And maybe somebody had figured out what they were planning, but – not knowing they were in fact lawmen in the employ of the United States Government – had mistaken them for real outlaws, and reported their activities to a marshal somewhere?

All of this was speculation. He couldn't easily stop and discuss things with Harbin, not with Lee Crane clinging on to him.

Ahead, the hills didn't seem to be getting any closer.

Harbin let Jericho and his passenger ride a little ahead, then he called over to one of his men, Jake

Wilmot. 'You and Henry drop back. Then, when that posse, whoever they are, catch up with you, show 'em your badges and tell them to go the hell back wherever they came from.'

The strangers had arrived in Red Rock a couple of days earlier, and Sheriff Longford had been told about them acting suspiciously. Simply the fact that the men kept themselves to themselves had been enough to cause gossip. But the clincher had been that, although the men had arrived in two separate groups, and although the men from the two groups kept well apart, it was clear to anybody with half an eye that they all knew each other.

'They're up to something,' Deputy Hawkins had said to Sheriff Longford the day before, looking out the window of the sheriff's office. They watched as a couple of the men from one group, who were walking down the street in one direction, took care to avoid a couple of the men from the other group as they walked down the street from the other direction.

'I figure they're all the same gang,' Longford had said. 'Instead of arriving in town all together, they've split into two groups, hoping that'd look less suspicious.'

'But they all know each other, that's for sure.'

'I'll tell you something else.'

'What's that, Sheriff?'

'That tall guy there – he's the boss. You can tell

how all the others treat him with respect, even when they're pretendin' they don't know who he is.'

'How you reckon that?'

'They turn their heads away to avoid looking him in the eye. He never does. He just keeps on looking straight ahead.'

Deputy Hawkins nodded. 'Yeah, I see it. But we still don't know what they're doin' here. Could they be meanin' to rob the bank?'

The sheriff rolled a cigarette, pushed it into his mouth, lit it. He blew a cloud of smoke up at the ceiling and said, 'Usually, bank robbers ride into town, rob the bank, and then ride out again. They don't all arrive in town a couple of days early and wait around, letting everybody get a good look at 'em. No, I reckon they're up to something else – and whatever it is, it's not going to happen in town. Close to town maybe, but not *in* town.'

'But there ain't anything close to town,' Hawkins said. 'It's all desert for miles around.'

'Don't forget the railroad,' said Sheriff Longford. 'You heard of any special cargoes being taken by rail in the next few days? A gold shipment – something like that?'

Hawkins shook his head. 'Not me, Sheriff.'

The sheriff thought a moment, then said, 'I think maybe I'll mosey on down to the telegraph office, send a couple of wires, see if anybody knows anything. . . .'

A little later he heard that a couple of prisoners

were being transferred to the state prison the next day, both of them due to hang. And one of them was Lee Crane, little brother of Walt Crane, wanted for murder in five states.

And as soon as the sheriff heard that, he figured he knew what the strangers were planning.

Jake and Henry dropped back to meet the posse, just as Harbin had told them. They were both US Cavalry men, who'd volunteered for this job. And because they were wearing civilian clothes, they'd been deputized, and issued with badges, so they could identify themselves if the need arose.

And it looked like that need was arising now.

They rode towards the oncoming posse, and when they were still a couple of hundred yards away, they stopped and took out their badges.

'Hold 'em up, good and high,' Jake said, 'so they can see 'em.'

So that's what he and Henry did.

Sweat broke out on Henry's forehead and ran into his eyes. Wiping away the sweat, he said, 'I wish somebody had told the local lawmen that we're just *pretending* to be outlaws.'

To which Jake said, 'This is supposed to be a secret mission. Nobody's supposed to know we're really on the side of the angels.'

'I know that,' said Henry. 'But even so. . . .'

He didn't get to finish the sentence. Just then a rifle bullet went clean through his chest and out the other side, spraying a jet of blood over the desert floor.

Sheriff Longford, riding at the head of his posse, Deputy Hawkins a little behind, saw the two riders break off from the group and head back towards them.

Hawkins shouted, 'A couple of them varmints are headin' back this way.'

'I see 'em,' said the sheriff. 'Get your rifle out. Soon as you're close enough, plug 'em.'

They knew now that the outlaws had helped the two convicted murderers – Lee Crane and another man – to escape from the train that had been taking them to prison. They'd seen the train derailed, the track torn up by an explosion. As they'd ridden past the train, the guards had waved and shouted at the posse, but the sheriff hadn't stopped. What could the guards tell them him that he didn't already know? You didn't have to be no genius to figure it out: Walt Crane and his gang had helped little brother Lee to escape, and they'd taken the other murdering varmint, too.

As they rode closer, the sheriff saw that the two men who'd broken off from the main pack were stopping. 'Looks like they're gonna make a stand,' yelled Hawkins.

Which was sure what it looked like.

Sheriff Longford's eyesight wasn't as good as it had once been, but it was good enough to see that the men each had something in his hand. And whatever they were holding glinted in the bright desert sunlight. 'They've drawn their guns,' he yelled back at Hawkins.

Hawkins was the best man with a rifle Longford had ever known. If he could see it, he could hit it.

He stopped his horse, gave it a moment to settle, then aimed his Springfield at the man on the left.

Hawkins fired. The noise of the shot rolled across the desert. A moment later, the man fell from his horse, a fountain of blood spouting from his back.

'Good shooting!' said one of the other deputies.

Sheriff Longford said, 'Now see if you can hit that other varmint.'

'Bet you a week's pay that I can,' said Hawkins, lining up his shot. But nobody took the bet.

A couple of hundred yards away, the remaining rider was waving his arms and yelling.

'What's he yellin'?' wondered the sheriff.

'I think he's yellin', "Don't shoot!" ' said one of the deputies.

'If he didn't want to get shot, he should've got himself an honest job,' said Sheriff Longford.

Hawkins had the second shot all lined up, his finger resting on the Springfield's trigger. 'You want me to shoot him, Sheriff?'

'Hell, yes,' said Sheriff Longford.

So Hawkins squeezed the trigger, and a moment later the man's head seemed to explode in a cloud of red.

'Right between the eyes!' said the sheriff admiringly.

Hawkins slid his rifle back into its scabbard and the posse set off again after the outlaws. And as they rode past the two dead men that Hawkins had shot, nobody saw that what the corpses were holding in their outstretched hands were silver badges, not guns.

Tom Jericho figured the rocks ahead of them were still the better part of a mile away.

To his left, Dan Harbin shouted, 'Those rocks are like a labyrinth. We can lose ourselves in there!'

We got to get there first, thought Jericho.

The first gunshot reached them, rolling across the desert and bouncing back at them off the hills.

Harbin twisted around in his saddle. He could see one of his men – Jake, he thought – still in his saddle, holding up his badge like he'd been told. The other man was on the ground and didn't seem to be moving. 'Sons of bitches have opened fire!' he yelled.

One of Harbin's men yelled, 'They've killed Henry!'

Then a second shot resounded through the hot air, and now there were two bodies on the ground, and two horses running scared and riderless across the desert.

'They've killed Jake!' shouted another of Harbin's men.

Harbin swore. He turned to Tom Jericho and yelled, 'You and your friend get to the rocks and hide out – the rest of us'll follow later!'

So with Lee Crane clinging to him, Jericho urged the horse onward toward the hills, while Harbin and his men hung back. And as he rode, Jericho thought: *What a goddamn mess!*

CHAPTER SIX

By the time Jericho – with Lee Crane clinging on to him – had reached the hills, he could already hear shots being exchanged behind him. A rifle bullet zinged past his ear and hit the side of a huge boulder before ricocheting off into the hills beyond. He didn't slow the horse till they were deep inside the natural labyrinth that was the red sandstone hills.

He slid off the horse and saw that Lee Crane was bleeding. A bullet had skimmed his leg, taking denim and skin with it. The blood was welling up in the wound, running down his boot and dripping to the ground, leaving a trail.

Lee's face was contorted with pain, but he wasn't whining; he hadn't even cried out when the bullet had sliced a groove in his flesh. Jericho wondered if maybe he'd underestimated the scrawny little guy all this time. Lee may be an outlaw and a convicted murderer, but he had guts.

Jericho helped Lee down off the horse. While Lee

sat on the ground, Jericho took his bandanna from around his own neck and tied it around Lee's shin. The bleeding slowed, then stopped altogether.

'Thanks,' said Lee.

They could hear gunfire from back out in the desert. Lots of it.

'You wait here,' said Jericho. 'I'll see what's happening.'

They were on a winding trail that gradually rose up into the hills, sandstone walls either side of them. Jericho scrambled up one of the walls. The climb was easier than it looked. He reached the top of the rock and peered over, keeping his head low.

Out in the desert, men in horseback were shooting at each other. Jericho couldn't tell who was who. The number of bodies lying motionless on the dust outnumbered the men still on horseback, shooting. As Jericho watched, the men continued to fire, till eventually there was only a couple of them left. . . .

Dan Harbin saw the posse ride towards them, all of them firing rifles now. He and his men were outnumbered. He considered giving the order to turn and run, but the thought only lasted a moment. They'd all be shot in the back long before they made it to the hills. 'Put your badges on!' he told his men.

One of his men said, 'That didn't do Jake and Henry no good!'

'Put 'em on anyway,' yelled Harbin.

So they all put their badges on – not that the posse

would be able to see them, not at that distance.

Harbin saw clouds of smoke billow from the posse riding towards them. The bullets zinged past them before the sound of the rifle shots reached them.

'God damn it!' said Collins, the man to Harbin's left.

'Get your hands up!' shouted Harbin.

'But they're shooting at us!'

'I told you to get your hands up!'

They all put their hands up. The posse continued riding towards them.

'We surrender!' shouted Harbin at the approaching men.

'We surrender!' shouted Collins.

The next moment a rifle bullet hit Collins in the chest and he fell from his horse, dead before he hit the dust.

'You damned sons of bitches!' screamed Harbin. 'Can't you see we're trying to surrender?'

In answer, a bullet nearly took off his ear.

'To hell with you, then!' he yelled. Turning to his men he said, 'Get out your rifles!'

Hawkins, the man who'd shot Jake and Henry, saw that the men they were chasing were putting their hands up. 'Looks like they're surrendering, Sheriff!' he yelled.

Sheriff Longford had been a lawman in one town or another for near thirty years. He remembered the time, back when he'd been a deputy, when he and the sheriff he was working for were chasing a gang of outlaws. The outlaws had pretended to surrender, and when young Deputy Longford and the sheriff had got closer, the outlaws had opened fire, killing the sheriff stone dead. Longford had learned a valuable lesson that day. Once a man crosses over to the wrong side of the law and chooses a path of evil, you can't trust him. Not even a little. There's no telling what he'll do. Several times since that occasion in Dodge, various outlaws had tried the same trick on him: pretended to surrender, then opened fire once he'd got close. But he'd been prepared, and they'd always come off worse. Outlaws had tried a lot of other tricks too, over the years, and Sheriff Longford knew most of them.

'They're trying to fool us,' said Sheriff Longford. 'Keep firing!'

They rode closer, and he could see that the outlaws were all wearing what appeared to be silver badges. But he knew this was a trick, too. He *knew* they were outlaws. That was definite.

They'd helped a couple of convicted murderers to escape, hadn't they?

He ordered his men to keep firing.

It was already clear that the man who'd shot Jake and Henry was the best rifle shot in the posse, so Harbin shouted, 'See the man with the red bandanna? Get him!'

So all of Harbin's men concentrated their fire on

the man who'd shot Jake and Henry, and eventually somebody got lucky. The fifteenth or sixteenth bullet blew off the man's Stetson, taking part of his skull with it.

Once they'd done that, Harbin told his men to fire at whoever the hell they wanted to fire at. And the men in the posse fired back. The posse had the advantage in numbers, but they were moving, and it's harder to shoot accurately from a galloping horse than it is from a standing one.

By the time the posse had got within a hundred yards of Harbin and his men, they were another five men down, whereas Harbin hadn't lost anymore. Which meant they were numbered about even.

Harbin took aim at the lead man and squeezed the trigger of his Winchester, but nothing happened. Just a click. So he had to dig into his saddle-bags for more cartridges and, as he was doing that, a bullet missed his head by about two inches.

Deciding he didn't have time to reload the Winchester, he let it drop from his hand and drew his Colt.

Harbin aimed at the lead man again, but, as he fired, his horse – scared by the posse approaching fast, now only about thirty, forty yards distant – shied away, giving out a startled whinny. The bullet missed the lead man and hit the fellow behind him instead, getting him square in the chest and knocking him off his horse.

Harbin shouted, 'We're on your side, you sons of

bitches!', but it didn't do any good. The posse either didn't hear, or didn't want to. He could see the silver badges glinting on their chests – couldn't the posse see *theirs?*

What the hell was wrong with them – were they blind?

He fired again at the lead man. This second bullet grazed the man's shoulder.

More gunshots rang out around them. More of the posse hit the dust, and now it was just the man who'd been in the lead, presumably the sheriff. Harbin looked around him, and his heart sank when he saw that he, too, was now alone.

Both men raised their guns, squeezing their triggers at the exact same moment. . . .

And both guns did nothing more than click as the hammers found only empty chambers. . . .

Each man made his own split-second decision. Sheriff Longford broke open his gun and pushed fresh cartridges into a chamber.

Dan Harbin drew his knife.

Sheriff Longford took aim at the outlaw's head.

The other man – the outlaw who had the almighty temerity to wear a lawman's badge – had taken out a knife and was riding towards him at full gallop.

The outlaw was yelling, but although Longford could see the man's mouth moving, the words were lost, drowned out by the noise of the sheriff's own blood thrumming in his ears.

Sheriff Longford was having trouble controlling his horse. It had got itself all steamed up and the sheriff couldn't hold it steady long enough to fire his bullets at the approaching outlaw.

With the man almost upon him, Sheriff Longford fired. Simultaneously, the outlaw lunged forward, slicing through the sheriff's throat.

Sheriff Longford thought he'd been punched in the neck. That's what it felt like. Then he saw the blood pouring out on to the front of his vest. He clamped his left hand over the wound, and with his right he aimed his pistol at the outlaw and fired.

Longford felt like he was floating, and his body felt cold, despite the desert sun. He felt himself slipping from out of his saddle, but he didn't feel the impact when he hit the ground. He never felt anything again.

Dan Harbin couldn't think. The world swung crazily around him. There was a deafening roar in his ears, and there was a searing pain running along one side of his head.

He knew that he had to get to the hills. Squinting through the haze of pain, and the blood that kept running into his eyes, he thought he could make out the shapes of the hills ahead of him, outlined against the sky.

He pointed his horse towards the rocks and urged the animal onwards.

CHAPTER SEVEN

Jericho clambered down the rock wall and went over to where Lee Crane was lying on the ground. It looked like his leg had stopped bleeding.

Jericho climbed on to the horse.

'You ain't running out on me, are you?' asked Lee.

'I won't be long,' said Jericho. He rode out through the narrow channel in the rocks and out into the desert.

Dan Harbin had almost reached the hills. Blood was still seeping out from the groove in the side of his head. He tried talking, but the words didn't make any sense. Jericho grabbed the reins of Dan's horse and led it into the channel in the rocks. At least there was some shade there.

They reached where Lee was now sitting upright against the rock wall. Jericho helped Harbin down from his horse and laid him out on the ground so he could get a good look at the wound.

Lee Crane said, 'My leg can keep a while, but that

fella needs a doctor fast, or he ain't gonna make it till tomorrow.'

Tom Jericho was inclined to agree. Untying the bandanna from Dan's neck, he retied it around the man's head. 'As I recall, there's a town fifty miles that way.' He nodded south. 'Cabot Springs.'

'We only have two horses,' said Lee. 'No food – and no water other than what's in the canteens. We can't stay here forever. Besides, sooner or later that posse is going to be missed. Which town you reckon they came from? You're from around here, I recall. You know this territory better than I do. . . .'

'There was a town back there – we passed through it on the train a while back. I forget the name.'

'It's closer,' said Lee, 'but we sure as hell can't go back that way. We better make for Cabot Springs.'

Tom Jericho looked at Harbin. He was delirious now, his mouth moving, but the words not audible. Yet. How soon before he said something that indicated to Lee Crane that the whole train escape had been playacting? 'I hate to move him,' said Jericho.

'We have no choice,' said Lee. 'He'll die if we stay here. And don't forget, we both owe our lives to that man. He saved us from the gallows. Least we can do is try to save him.'

Jericho cursed under his breath. Tricking Lee Crane would come a lot easier, he figured, if Crane acted like a murdering son of a bitch was supposed to act, instead of turning noble when you least expected it.

Jericho saw that Dan's head wound wasn't bleeding so fast now. 'OK,' he said. 'We'll wait here in the shade, just till the day cools a little. Then we'll head to Cabot Springs. By the time we get there, it'll be dark. There'll be less chance of being seen by anybody who's inclined to cause a fuss.'

'It's a better plan than anything I can think up,' said Lee Crane. He rested his head on the cool sandstone wall. He breathed in deeply, then exhaled. 'Don't that taste great?'

'What tastes great?' asked Jericho.

'Freedom,' said Lee.

They set off a couple of hours later, the sun sinking over towards the west and casting longer and longer shadows as they rode.

Working together, they hauled the semi-conscious Dan Harbin up on to one of the horses. Jericho climbed up in front of him, and then tied Dan's arms around his waist to keep him upright. Lee took the other horse.

It was slow going. About five hours after they'd started out, with the western sky now a blaze of red and orange as the sun travelled beyond the horizon, Lee rode up to Jericho and said, 'You look dog-tired. You want me to take our friend from here on? We must've gone more than halfway by now.'

And once again, Jericho wondered if maybe he'd misjudged Crane. If he hadn't known better, Jericho might have started the think the guy wasn't so bad.

But then, Crane *had* been convicted of murder, hadn't he?

'I'll be OK for a while,' said Jericho.

To which Lee Crane said, 'OK, but if you want me to take him, just say the word.'

'I sure will,' replied Jericho.

Another hour or so later, Harbin started to mumble in his delirium. This time around, some of the words were distinct. Some of them even linked up, and started to make sense.

'Yes sir, Mr Governor,' murmured Dan. 'We'll get those Crane boys for you . . . Whatever they're up to, you can be sure we'll put a stop to it. . . .'

'Hush now, Dan,' said Jericho. He looked over to Lee Crane, some twenty feet away to the left. The sun had gone down now, but the moon was shining like burnished silver, and Jericho could see Crane clearly enough. Had Crane heard what Dan had said? He didn't give any indication that he had, but that didn't necessarily mean anything.

Dan started talking again.

'*Shhh!*' said Jericho.

Then Lee Crane pointed ahead of them and said, 'I can see a light!'

Jericho couldn't see any light. He was about to tell Crane that it must be wishful thinking, but then he saw the light too – a flicker of an oil lamp, maybe. And then there was another light, and another.

'You see 'em?' asked Crane, almost jumping out of his saddle with excitement.

'I see 'em,' said Jericho.

'We must be nearing the town!'

Behind Jericho, Dan Harbin said, 'We'll get 'em, Mr Governor!'

'What did he say?' asked Crane.

'Just rambling,' said Jericho. 'It don't mean nothing.'

It took them another couple of hours to reach Cabot Springs. And in that time, Dan Harbin didn't say anything more. Nobody did.

They reached the edge of town, and found a house with a shingle hanging outside it that read: MORGAN SIMMS, DENTAL SURGEON.

'I figure a dentist is close enough to a doctor,' said Jericho.

The dentist's house was in darkness. It stood isolated within a neat little fenced-in yard. The closest building was sixty, seventy feet away.

Jericho and Lee Crane climbed down from their horses, and together they lifted Harbin to the ground. Crane said to Jericho, 'You better do the talking. People don't seem to like my face. I'll hold our friend.'

So leaving Crane holding Dan upright, Jericho opened the gate in the white-painted fence and knocked on the door of the dentist's house.

While the dentist tended to Dan Harbin, his wife – who doubled as his nurse – tended to Crane's leg wound in the adjoining room.

After he'd done what he could for Dan, the dentist told Jericho, 'I guess I don't have to tell you, your friend with the head wound won't be able to travel for several days, maybe not even weeks.'

'But he'll live?' asked Jericho.

'He was lucky. The bullet only grazed his skull. He'll live, and so far as I can tell, there isn't any damage to his brain. With luck he'll be good as new in a few months. I've sedated him, so he'll be sleeping for awhile. As for your other friend – the one with the leg wound – he should be able to move around in a day or so.'

Jericho nodded. 'Thanks, but I don't think he or I will want to stick around that long. My friend with the sore head will have to stay here. . . . We'd all appreciate it you didn't tell anybody about our visit – not till my friend's woken up, anyway. And when he wakes up, I'm sure he'll arrange for you to be paid in full.'

The dentist didn't know what to make of any of this, so he nodded and said, 'I guessed by the nature of the wounds that—'

Whatever he was going to say was lost, because he was interrupted by a shriek from the next room. Jericho burst through the door, the dentist behind him.

The first thing Jericho saw was the dentist's wife – an attractive woman, about thirty years old – squeezing herself into one corner of the room, and a look of terror on her face. The second thing he saw was Lee Crane sitting on the edge of a bed, grinning and saying, 'Damn it, Tom – I thought she *wanted* me to touch her!'

And at that moment Jericho figured maybe Lee Crane was still at least nine-tenths snake after all. He hit Lee on the point of the chin, hard. Lee's head snapped back and he slumped back on to the bed, unconscious.

'I want you take him out of here, *now*!' yelled the dentist.

'We're just on our way,' said Tom Jericho, hauling Lee up on to his shoulder and carrying him from the room.

'What the hell did you hit me for?' asked Lee. 'I thought we were friends!'

These were the first words he said when he woke up, tied across the back of his horse.

By this time, they were several miles south of Cabot Springs.

Jericho said, 'If I hadn't hit you, I doubt if I could've persuaded the dentist and his wife not to go screaming for the sheriff as soon as we'd gone. But hitting you seemed to satisfy 'em. For a while, anyways.'

'But we didn't even get chance to eat,' complained Lee. 'I'm hungry!'

'You expected them to feed us after what you did?'

'I couldn't help myself. She looked so good.'

'Bull. There ain't ever any excuse for touching a woman when she don't want to be touched. And don't try and tell me you thought she wanted you to, because that's bull too. You *wanted* to think she wanted you to touch her, and that's a very different thing.'

If Lee understood the difference, he didn't spend much time pondering it, because he said, 'You gonna untie me? What you tie me up like this for, anyway?'

'So you didn't fall off the damn horse,' Jericho told him. 'Why d'you think?'

'Uh – oh yeah,' said Lee.

He never was too bright, thought Jericho, getting off his horse and untying Lee.

Once Lee was down off his horse, he started complaining again. 'I'm hungry!' he whined.

'The doc and his wife gave us food,' said Jericho. 'Bread and cold meat.' This had been a really kind gesture from them, Jericho figured. The dentist and his wife must be real, died-in-the-wool Good People, giving food to people whom they must have known were outlaws, and one of whom couldn't keep his damned hands to himself. Jericho hadn't even told them that he and Dan Harbin were really working for the government, pretending to be outlaws to fool Crane. He'd wanted to tell them, but that would have been way too risky.

'Bread and cold meat?' said Lee. 'Is that all?'

Jericho resisted the impulse to hit him again. Only a little while ago he'd been thinking that maybe he'd got Lee Crane all wrong – or maybe that he'd changed since they'd been in prison together, all those years ago. But now Jericho figured Lee hadn't changed. He was the same squirming little snake he'd been back then, only older.

And Jericho figured he knew the real reason why Lee had offered to take his turn minding Dan Harbin on the long night ride to Cabot Springs – it wasn't out of the goodness of his heart, but so he could ingratiate himself with Jericho.

The truth now shone plain as day: Lee Crane went through life being taken care of by somebody or other, usually his brother. But if his brother wasn't about, Lee found somebody else to take care of him. In state prison it had, briefly, been Jericho. And now it was Jericho again.

Which suited the plan perfectly, but the realization that he was expected to act as nursemaid to this mean-spirited son of a bitch grated on Jericho's nerves.

Lee said, 'I vote we go back there, tie 'em up, and get ourselves some real food!'

I vote I hit you again, thought Jericho. *I vote to I keep hitting you till I've either beaten some sense into you, or you don't get up again, ever.* But he didn't say that. Instead he said, 'So far we've been luckier than we deserve. Going back would be pushing our luck way too far.'

Even Lee, dumb as he was, seemed to accept the truth of that. Sulkily he said, 'So where's the damn bread and cold meat?'

Jericho dug the food out from his saddle-bag and gave some to Lee.

At least that kept him quiet for a while. It gave his mouth something to do, other than moan. But all good things come to an end. Eventually he swallowed the last morsel of bread, got up off the rock he'd been sitting on and said, 'We're still wearing prison clothes.'

'I know,' said Jericho.

'We shoulda taken some of the doc's clothes,' said Lee.

'I don't know if you noticed,' said Jericho, 'but the doc was shorter than either of us, and a lot rounder. If we'd tried wearing his clothes, anybody seeing us would tell right away they were stolen.'

'Guess you're right,' agreed Lee, scratching his chin. Then he said, 'Did he give us any money?'

'Nope,' sighed Jericho. 'He didn't. And I didn't ask for none. I was just grateful for the food and the doctoring, and the promise he'd give us a head start before he told anybody we'd been there.'

Lee stood on the rock he'd been sitting on and peered back the way they'd come. The sun was up again, low in the east, casting long, long shadows across the desert. A few miles back, a couple or three ribbons of smoke rose up into the clear blue sky, dead straight, not so much as a breath of wind disturbing them. Some of the gentlefolk of Cabot Springs were early risers.

'Maybe we shoulda killed 'em,' murmured Lee.

Jericho controlled his temper. Keeping his voice even, he said, 'And what do you suppose would happen when somebody gets a toothache and goes to the dentist for help? Town that size, somebody'd be bound to go see the dentist sometime today – and then we'd get a fresh posse on our tail.'

Lee shrugged. 'What the hell. I don't see anybody following us. Maybe the doc's good as his word after all. . . . Where we going, anyway?'

'Over the border,' said Jericho. 'I don't know where Dan Harbin was planning to take us. If he had a hideout in mind, he didn't tell me about it. So I figured the best thing we can do is cross into Mexico, the border being so close. If we think of a better plan, we can always cross back this side of the border again.'

Lee jumped down off the rock. 'Sounds good to me,' he said. 'How far is the border?'

'Sixty miles,' said Jericho. 'There or thereabouts.'

'*Sixty miles?*' complained Lee. 'That's a day's ride – more, maybe.'

'If you want, I could hit you again,' Jericho told him. 'You can sleep part of the way.'

'No thanks,' said Lee.

Jericho got on to his horse. 'And if you were wondering about the horses, they were fed and watered while you were sleeping.'

'I didn't even think about the damned horses,' said Lee.

Of course you didn't, thought Jericho. *You only ever*

think about yourself. 'Get mounted,' he said. 'Sooner we start, sooner we get there.'

'When we get to Mexico,' said Lee, climbing up on to his horse, 'we should go join my brother. Last I heard, he and the rest of the gang were in Sonora territory.'

Jericho had been told that Walt Crane was some-where around the Arizona-Mexico border, but nobody knew exactly where. 'Sonora, huh? That's fine by me. But Sonora's a big place. You know where he's liable to be?'

'We got a hideout down there,' Lee told him. 'Our own hacienda. You'll like it.'

'I'm sure I will,' said Tom Jericho. 'Sonora it is, then. I'd sure like to meet your brother. I've heard a lot about him.'

CHAPTER EIGHT

Night had fallen by the time Jericho and Lee reached a town again. It was called Jacobsville and was some five miles from the border. It wasn't a big town, but it was big enough to have a saloon. They could hear music playing: a harmonica, and somebody trying to saw all the way through a fiddle, and taking their time about it. That was over the other side of town. Jacobsville wasn't as big as Cabot Springs had been. On paydays, when the cowboys came to town to spend their wages, the population probably near doubled.

This side of town was quiet. A little past midnight, and no lights anywhere. They were at one end of a short street that looked to be mostly residences, apart from a general store, but nothing stirred.

They tied their horses to a rail and wandered in the direction of the music, not heading straight for the store in case anybody was watching from a window. But once they'd passed the storefront, they ducked into an alleyway and made their way around towards the rear of the store.

Both Jericho and Lee knew that the storekeeper – maybe a whole family – would most likely be upstairs in the living quarters, so they'd have to do everything in as close to total silence as they could manage.

The back door was bolted from the inside. There was a window next to it, the kind with a latch holding the upper and lower halves together. Lee dug a penknife from his pocket, slid it into the gap between the two halves, and opened the latch. He grinned at Jericho. 'Easy when you know how,' he said.

Jericho said, 'Where'd you get the knife?'

'I borrowed it from our sleeping friend.'

He meant Dan Harbin.

'You take anything else?'

'No,' replied Lee, sounding as if he was offended by the notion, adding, 'I'm sure he won't mind me using it for a while. I'll give it back the next time I see him.' He closed the blade and slipped the penknife back into his pocket. Lee inched the bottom half of the sash window upwards, making only the slightest scraping noise, till he'd raised it enough for him to crawl through.

Jericho followed. When they were both inside the store they stood still for a moment, letting their eyes adjust. With the moonlight pouring in through the big glass window at the front of the store, it was only a matter of seconds before they were able to move around without knocking into anything.

'Clothes are over here,' whispered Lee.

Jericho went over to him and saw there were shelves of work shirts and jeans and coats. There were Stetsons too – fresh from the factory, the crowns round and high and the brims straight, waiting for the buyer to steam and roll and fold the hat into whatever shape he chose.

The store sold guns, too. They each picked out a six-gun, loaded it, and set about choosing a holster. Jericho noticed that Lee Crane spent longer choosing a holster that he'd spent choosing a gun – which he figured just about said it all.

Finding a carpetbag, Jericho dumped a few boxes of .45 calibre cartridges into it, some cans of beans and salted pork, and tobacco and a few other items. *If I'm going to playact the role of an outlaw,* he thought, *I may as well do it properly.*

They were making their way back to the open window when a voice shouted, 'Hold it right there, you thieving sons of bitches!'

The voice was deep and full of anger. 'Get your hands up and turn around to face me, real slow!'

They did as they were told.

A man stood on the stairs leading up to the living quarters. He was tall and burly, and he held a Colt .45 aimed at them.

Jericho figured they must have roused the man from his slumbers. He must've got out of bed and pulled on the pants he was wearing, grabbed his gun and descended halfway down the stairs, all without making a noise. Which Jericho thought mighty impressive. The fella sure moved quietly for a man his size.

'So that's what a pair of lowdown skunks looks like,' said the man. 'I always wondered.'

To Jericho's surprise, Lee grinned at the man. 'Now, you caught us stealin' fair and square, but I don't see no cause for you to start insultin' us!'

The big man's face twisted with rage, and in the moonlight it seemed to get a shade or two darker. 'You damn varmint,' he said, levelling his gun at Lee. 'I oughta plug you!'

'But you won't,' said Lee.

'What?' said the man.

'You won't shoot,' said Lee. 'You're a tenderfoot. You're from back East, I can tell it in your voice.'

'So?' demanded the man.

'If you'd been born and raised out West, I'd figure you'd shoot. But not with you being from the East. You may have come out here some time ago, but you're still a tenderfoot – I can tell. You're one of them law-abiding, go-to-church-on-Sundays kind of folks. You talk big, but you ain't never shot nobody in your life. I'm right, ain't I?'

The man blinked, and swallowed hard. No one had ever spoken to him like this before. He'd gone through life scaring people, and he'd not needed a gun to do it. Usually all he had to do was look at a man oddly, they backed down. But here and now, things weren't happening the way they were supposed to. 'Sure I have,' he said.

'Sure you have, *what?*' said Lee.

'Shot a man.'

'The hell you have. And that gives you a problem.'

The storekeeper cocked the hammer of his Colt and pointed it right between Lee's eyes. 'It ain't me who's got a problem,' he said.

Lee's grin got even broader. 'Yes you have. You ain't never shot nobody, and you ain't never *killed* nobody, and we both know it. Which means you don't know how you're gonna feel, day after day, looking at yourself in the mirror, knowing you've killed a man.'

And it was about then that Jericho, who'd been wondering what Lee was up to, began to see there might be method in this madness. The storekeeper's initial rush of anger was ebbing away, and was being replaced – moment by moment – by doubt and fear. Jericho could see it in the man's eyes.

'You son of a bitch,' said the storekeeper, trying to get his anger to rise up again. But the muzzle of his pistol was wavering.

And now that Lee had the big man off-balance, he figured it was time to draw his own gun.

Out of the corner of his eye, Jericho saw Lee's hand move towards his holster. Jericho kicked out, sweeping Lee's feet out from beneath him. Lee's finger tightened on the trigger as he fell backwards, his gun firing a bullet harmlessly into the floor.

Reacting to the gunshot, the storeowner also fired, sending a bullet zinging over Lee's head and crashing through the store's window.

Jericho drew his gun, but didn't fire it. Hefting it by the barrel, he threw the pistol at the storeowner's head. The distance wasn't more than ten feet, and Jericho's skill at throwing knives served him well. The butt of the spinning revolver connected with the man's skull, stunning him. As the big man swayed, Jericho ran at him and delivered an uppercut to his jaw, knocking him cold.

Jericho scooped his gun up off the floor and pushed it back into his holster. Meanwhile, Lee was pushing himself up on to his feet, saying, 'Why'd you do that?'

'I just saved your life,' Jericho told him. 'If I hadn't kicked your legs out from under you, he would've shot you in the head.'

'Naw,' whined Lee, 'I woulda shot him first. Didn't you see how shook up I'd got him?'

Jericho grabbed the carpetbag containing the ammunition and tins of food and the rest. 'Never mind that now,' he said. 'We'd better get out of here and across the border before any lawmen show up. Don't forget, you've promised to introduce me to your brother. I'm sure looking forward to it. I ain't never met anybody famous before.'

Lee Crane led Tom Jericho across the border. Another hour's ride and they arrived at a farmstead.

The main house was a long, wide hacienda, white-washed and cool-looking in the Mexican sunshine.

They left their horses in the shade, and Lee shouted through the open front door, '*Hola*! Anybody home?'

An old woman dressed all in black, almost bent double with age, pottered out of the shadows. In a heavy accent she said, 'Who's there?'

Lee said, 'It's me, Lopita – Lee!'

Suddenly the old woman seemed to shed a few years. She uncurled her back and shot Lee a broad grin. 'Mister Lee! You're here!' Then she looked past him at Jericho, and past Jericho and into the empty front yard and said, 'But where is your brother and the rest of the gang?'

Lee shrugged. 'Don't ask me, Lopita. I just got here.'

The woman frowned. 'But your brother, Mr Walt – he and the rest of the gang, they go north to Arizona, to help you escape from the train. . . .'

'They *what*?' exclaimed Lee.

Listening to all of this, Tom Jericho didn't know whether to laugh or cry. The plan had been for Dan Harbin and his men – posing as outlaws – to help him and Lee escape from the train, in the hope that Lee would then take Jericho to Walt. But if what the woman said was true, Harbin and his men needn't have bothered faking the escape. Walt and his gang would have grabbed Lee anyway, and possibly taken Jericho with them as well.

Jericho thought of all the men who'd died on account of this dumb plan he'd got himself involved in, and felt a little sick.

Lee turned to Jericho. 'Looks like we might as well relax for a while. We ain't got nothing else to do except wait for my brother to come back.'

Jericho nodded. 'Sure looks that way,' he said.

Dan Harbin opened his eyes. A woman was mopping his brow with a damp cloth. The first thing he said was, 'What happened?'

The woman said, 'A bullet grazed your skull. You're lucky to be alive.'

'Sounds like it,' he agreed. 'Am I in a hospital?'

'No,' she said. 'My husband is a dentist. Your friends brought you here. We told them there were doctors in Cabot Springs, but they were quite insistent my husband treat you, despite him not being familiar with bullet wounds and. . . .' She bit her lip, thinking maybe she'd said too much in her nervousness.

Harbin said, 'You say a bullet grazed my skull?'
She nodded.

'I don't remember a damn thing.'

'About how you come to be here, or about getting shot?' she asked.

He said, 'I mean, I don't remember anything about *anything*.'

That wasn't quite true. He could remember ambushing a train, with a number of men who were under his command. He could remember that on the train were two men – Dan couldn't remember their names – and that if he didn't rescue them, they were going to be hanged.

And he remembered something else: men with silver badges pinned to their chests, opening fire and killing all his men.

Other than that, his life seemed to be pretty much a blank. He had vague recollections of childhood. He knew, somehow, that his name was Daniel Harbin, and that he'd been raised in Texas.

But it looked like the bullet that had nearly taken his head off hadn't only cut a groove in his skull: it had also torn out a chunk of his memories.

He reached out and caught hold of the woman's wrist. 'Level with me,' he said. 'Am I. . . ?'

The woman's eyes widened. 'Are you what?' she asked him.

'Am I an outlaw?'

'Yes,' she said. 'You're an outlaw. Your two friends were due to be hanged for murder, but you helped them escape.'

I'm an outlaw, thought Dan. 'Where are they?' he asked, raising his head and looking around, as if they might be hiding in the corner of the room.

'They left yesterday. They didn't say where they were going, but I expect they've crossed into Mexico. We're only a few miles from the border.'

Dan realized he was still holding the woman's wrist. One thing he could never abide was men who maltreated womenfolk. He released his grip. 'Sorry,' he said. 'I didn't hurt you, did I?'

'No,' she said.

But he saw that he'd left a red mark encircling her wrist, and he felt bad about it.

Mexico, Dan thought. I guess if I'm an outlaw and that's where my friends have gone, maybe I'd better head down to Mexio too.

CHAPTER NINE

Bob Feeney, his ear pressed against the rail, said, 'Train ain't coming, Walt.'

Walt and his gang had been waiting most of the day, waiting to ambush the train carrying his brother to prison. The train should have reached this point on its route over an hour earlier, and now here was Bob Feeney saying he couldn't even hear its approach through the goddamn rail. Walt spat, got down on his knees and listened for himself.

Nothing.

'God damn it!' he said, wondering if the man who'd given him the information about the train had been wrong. 'If Calhoun sold me a bum steer, I'll. . . .'

'Take a look at this, Walt,' said Billy Stanhope. Billy was peering way off into the horizon at something, his hands shielding his eyes from the glare of the desert sun.

'What?' asked Walt, getting up off the dirt.

'Smoke,' said Billy.

'You mean *steam?*' asked Walt, wishing his eyes were as young as Billy's.

'Nope,' said Billy. 'I mean smoke.'

'I see it too,' said another member of the gang. 'That's smoke, all right.'

Walt and his men rode off to investigate. And after a couple of hours' riding they discovered that somebody had ambushed the train already, and that Lee had gone.

There were tracks leading south. They followed the tracks, and it wasn't too long before they saw vultures circling in the sky up ahead.

When they got up close they saw a mass of bodies lying in the dirt. Some of the bodies had silver badges pinned to their chests. Others were holding badges in their hands, or the badges were on the ground close by. Walt didn't ponder too much on this. He just figured they were all lawmen, and that was that.

Walt told his men, 'We better get out of here before somebody else shows up, and they think we killed 'em.'

By now it was close to sundown, and they'd been out in the heat all day, so Walt said, 'We'll rest in them hills over there. At sun-up we'll start riding again.'

Which suited everybody just fine. They were heading south, following the direction Lee had gone, and they all knew that Walt had been planning to go south anyway, to do a job.

Nobody except Walt knew what the job was. All anybody else knew – or *thought* they knew – was that they'd been hired to do something down in Mexico, in the state of Sonora. They didn't know who'd hired them, or what they'd been hired to do, but everybody figured it must have something to do with the revolution that had been rumbling away down there for some time.

The next morning they continued south till they got to Cabot Springs. They rode into town and found the saloon. Walt and his men bought themselves some bottles of whiskey, then Walt said to the bartender, 'You seen this fella?'

He pulled a folded paper from his vest pocket and opened it out, smoothing it flat on the bar. It was a Wanted poster. On it was a fairly recognizable drawing of his brother.

The bartender's usual answer to such a question would have been along the lines of, 'Who wants to know?' But something about the man asking him, and the men he was with, told the barman that his usual answer was liable to get him shot. So he said, 'I ain't seen him.' Which was true.

Standing next to Walt, Ned Grimes pulled his gun and pointed it at the bartender's head. 'You sure about that?'

There were a few other people in the saloon, apart from Walt and his gang. They all went quiet.

Walt turned to Ned. 'Now that ain't nice,' he told Ned. 'I'm sure our friend here has already figured out that if he lies to me, I'm gonna tie him butt-naked to a horse and ride him around in the desert till his hide's been stripped off him.' He turned to look at the bartender. 'You *had* figured that out, hadn't you?'

The bartender nodded. 'Yes sir.'

'Good,' said Walt. 'I'll just ask you the same question one more time, just to be sure you understood it right. Are you sure you ain't seen this fella?' He tapped the poster.

'I'm sure,' croaked the bartender, his throat tight.

Walt Crane turned back to Ned. 'Ask all these other folk in here if they've seen Lee. I'll be right here at the bar, drinkin' whiskey.'

It took Ned a little while to be satisfied that all the other saloon customers were telling the truth when they told him they hadn't seen Lee. By the time he'd finished, Walt was sitting at a table with a fresh bottle of whiskey in front of him.

Ned sat down opposite him. 'They ain't seen him.'

Walt didn't ask if Ned was sure they were telling the truth, because Walt knew that Ned wouldn't have said so if he wasn't sure. Instead Walt said, 'You know, we should be going about this more scientifically.'

'*Scientifically?*'

'We ain't been thinking straight. There was a lot of shooting out there, right? What with all them lawmen lying around, and all. . . .'

'Yeah,' agreed Ned.

'So what if Lee, or somebody he was with, got hurt? They'd find a doctor, right?'

'Right,' agreed Ned.

Walt poured himself another drink. 'So I reckon we should find out where the closest doctor is. I think we should pay him a visit.'

There wasn't just one doctor in Cabot Springs, but two. Both of the doctors swore they'd never set eyes on the man in the poster.

'So what do we do now?' Ned asked Walt that night, when they and the rest of the gang were all back in the saloon. The gang had the place to themselves, having scared everybody else away.

'I'm thinkin' about it,' replied Walt, slurring his words a little. They served good whiskey in this place, and he and his men appreciated good whiskey.

They sat for a while longer, not talking, just drinking and smoking, till eventually the silence was broken by Ned, who cursed, his hand going up to his mouth.

'What the hell's wrong with you?' Walt asked. Ned was probing deep inside his mouth with his finger. 'God damned tooth again,' he said.

'You need to get that tooth pulled,' Walt said.

'I don't wanna get it pulled. I only got half the number of teeth I started out with, and I don't wanna lose any more, or I won't be able to chew worth a damn.'

'So get yourself some dentures,' said Walt.

'I don't want dentures,' Ned complained. 'I want my own teeth, not some false set o' jaws I gotta keep putting in and taking out.'

Walt shrugged and poured himself another slug of the good whiskey. 'OK, so keep the damned tooth. But if you do, you gotta stop whining like a little girl or I'll get some pliers and pull it out myself!'

Which shut Ned up for a while, because as big and mean as Ned was, he was mighty scared of Walt. Something else he was scared of was the idea of getting his tooth pulled, which was the real reason he didn't want to do anything about his aching tooth. But he was more scared of Walt's anger than he was of getting his tooth pulled, so a couple of minutes later he said, 'Maybe I should find myself a dentist. He could give me the gas. You ever had the gas?'

Walt said no, he'd never had the gas. But he also said he thought it was a good idea for Ned to find himself a dentist.

So Ned asked the bartender where he could find a dentist, and the bartender told him there was a dentist on the northern edge of town.

Both of the doctors had been situated close to the centre of town. Overhearing the bartender, it occurred to Walt that, if somebody trying to outrun the law was injured, they'd be more likely to try and get help from a dentist located on the edge of town than from a doctor located in the middle. There'd be less chance of being seen.

That's what *he'd* do, anyway.

'Let's go find that dentist,' said Walt, rising out of his chair. But when he tried to stand on his own two feet, he lost his balance and crashed back down again. 'I'm drunker than I thought,' he said. 'Maybe – maybe I better have myself a little sleep first. We can visit the dentist in the morning. . . .'

The sun had risen high, and the shadows had short-ened to almost nothing by the time Walt opened his eyes. Somehow he'd made the journey from the saloon to one of the bedrooms on the floor above.

He was still dressed though, and still wore his boots and gunbelt, and was lying on top of the bed, not in it. His hat was perched on one of the brass bed knobs.

Walt hauled himself off the bed, splashed water on his face, put on his hat and left the room.

He found Ned still down in the saloon, lying flat on his back, mouth open, on top of the table where they'd been drinking. Walt drank some whiskey to dull the pain in his head a little, then poured a little into Ned's mouth.

Ned spluttered and woke up.

'Here,' said Walt, handing him the bottle, which still had a couple of inches of booze in it. 'There's your breakfast. Get your hat. We're gonna talk to that dentist.'

It was another hot day again outside. Walt couldn't remember the last time he'd felt rain.

Dan Harbin's plan was to wait till the dentist had inspected his head again and redressed his wound, then continue south to Mexico and see if he could catch up with those friends of his who'd brought him to Cabot Springs. He still couldn't remember much, but he thought one of his friends' names was Lee Crane. He thought the other might be called Jericho, something like that.

He had no idea how he was going to find Lee Crane and Jericho, other than just asking everybody he met. He seemed to be able to speak some Spanish, which would help. But even if he had little chance of finding them, crossing into Mexico was a good idea anyway. He was an outlaw, and he'd evidently been in a gunfight, probably with lawmen – and maybe he'd even killed a lawman himself? In which case, hanging around in Arizona would be just plain stupid.

How he was going to travel was another matter. His friends hadn't left him a horse. The dentist's wife had told him that the three of them had arrived on only two horses, and they'd taken them both. Had his own horse been killed in the gunfight? He couldn't remember. Maybe he'd have to steal one. Horse-stealing was a hanging crime, but if he was going to get hanged for murdering a lawman anyway. . . .

'Your wound's clearing up about as well as can be expected,' said the dentist, after looking at the injury. 'Of course, I've no idea what damage there might be to your brain. Even a regular doctor wouldn't be able to tell you that. You still can't remember much?'

'Not much,' said Harbin, as the dentist's wife – whose name, he now knew, was Mary – dressed his head with a fresh white bandage. 'Couple of things have come back to me, but mostly my past is a blank.'

'I wish I could tell you your memories aren't lost forever,' the dentist told him. 'But I can't.' He lapsed into silence for a moment, then he said, 'You sure you're an outlaw? You don't act like one. You ain't got a mean bone in your body.'

Dan Harbin grinned. 'Thanks for that. But I can't be sure if I'm an outlaw or not. By the sounds of it, the men who brought me here were outlaws, so I guess that makes me an outlaw too. And if we weren't on the wrong side of the law, why didn't they take me to one of those doctors in town? Why else would they leave me here, with a dentist who lives on the edge of town, where there are fewer people to see who comes and goes? That and the bullet scraping my head – it all adds up to me being an outlaw, don't it? Maybe getting a head wound has changed me? I seem to recall I've heard of such things happening. Maybe before I got shot I was the meanest son of a gun in the West, but all the meanness got knocked out of me. . . . Who knows? I sure don't. But what I *do* know is, it don't seem like a good idea to wait around and see if anybody wants to hang me.'

The dentist nodded. 'I have to tell you, travelling

isn't going to be good for your health right now. But, as you've just pointed out, sticking around very likely wouldn't be very good for your health either. . . . I guess you'll be wanting this. . . .'

The dentist went to a drawer, opened it, and lifted something out. He held it out for Dan to take.

It was a single-shot derringer pistol, secured in an undersized holster with a leather strap.

'This was on your right leg, just above your boot,' the dentist told him.

Dan took the little gun and fixed it to his leg. 'Thanks, Doc. If it weren't for you and your wife, I—' He was interrupted by somebody knocking on the front door.

'I'll see who that is,' said Mary, hurrying out of the room.

The two men waited in silence, listening. They heard Mary open the door, and her light voice saying, 'May I help you?'

They didn't hear anything else till two men pushed their way into the room a couple of seconds later, the bigger man holding Mary tight around the waist with one hand, his other hand clamped over her mouth.

The smaller, meaner-looking man held a Wanted poster. He showed it to the dentist and to Dan Harbin. 'You seen him?' he asked.

'Let go of my wife!' yelled the dentist.

The man with the poster slugged the dentist across the chin. Not hard enough to knock him cold, just

83

hard enough to keep him in line. He held the poster out again. 'You seen him?' he said again.

Harbin saw the drawing on the poster, and the name: LEE CRANE.

Whoever these men were, Harbin figured they weren't law. They looked like the kind of men who'd get at the truth eventually and didn't care much who they hurt. Dan Harbin figured he owed the dentist and his wife Mary a lot, and he didn't want them getting hurt just because he'd held out on these men. 'I know Lee Crane,' he said. 'They were carrying him to state prison, by train. I helped him escape. I was injured. He and another man – name of Jericho – brought me here.'

Rubbing his jaw, the dentist said, 'They've gone. They didn't say where they were going, but we think they've gone south. To Mexico.'

The man with the poster grinned. He turned to the other man, the one with his arm clamped around Mary's waist. 'See? That's what happens when you start thinkin' *scientifically*!'

CHAPTER TEN

Walt Crane held out his hand. 'I'm Walt Crane, and I owe you a big thanks.'

'Dan Harbin,' said Dan, shaking the man's hand. 'Now, d'you think your friend would stop manhandling that lady?'

Ned Grimes let the woman go.

Walt said, 'We're headin' down to Mexico. You want to come with us?'

'I reckon,' said Dan.

That afternoon Walt Crane and his gang – with Harbin tagging along – left Cabot Springs, heading for the border.

Harbin was riding the dentist's horse. When he'd told Walt Crane that he didn't have a mount, the dentist had said, 'Take mine', knowing that if he didn't offer it, they'd take it anyway.

Nevertheless, when they were alone a few minutes later, Dan had said to the dentist, 'As soon as I can I'll return the horse to you, or replace it, or pay you a fair price for it.'

The dentist had nodded, but even though he'd wanted to believe Harbin, he thought it probable he'd never see the horse again – or a replacement, or any money.

Harbin had felt bad about taking the horse, but sticking around would have likely resulted in him getting strung up from a tree. So he'd taken it.

As he rode south with Walt and his gang of outlaws, Dan could feel his memories lurking somewhere in the darker corners of his mind, just out of reach. It seemed like they were calling to him, trying to tell him something, but he couldn't quite make out the words.

The gang didn't make it to Jacobsville till long after night had fallen. As usual, their intention was to make straight for the nearest saloon, but, as they passed through the town, Walt noticed that wooden boards had been nailed over the front of a general store, where a glass window should have been.

The boards looked fresh; it occurred to Walt that his brother Lee was just about incapable of passing through a town without breaking something, so maybe this storefront with the missing window was down to him.

He told Ned Grimes to hang back, and sent the rest of his men to the saloon – and by this time they knew there *was* a saloon, because they could hear the music, or what passed for music, wafting out at them from across the other side of town.

Dan Harbin had been riding along a little behind Ned, so he stopped also, and said to Walt, 'Something the matter?'

Walt nodded to the boarded-up storefront. 'Just about every day of his life, my little brother has broken or killed something. He can't help it. It was the way he was made, I guess. So when I saw that storefront, I started wonderin' if maybe the store-keeper knows something about Lee.'

So they all tied up their horses, and Walt banged on the door loud enough to stir a corpse.

They didn't have to wait long. Not more than about five seconds later, a window opened above them and an angry-looking man leaned out. His head had a bandage wrapped around it.

Ned Grimes turned to Dan, a big grin on his face, and said, 'He's got a bandage round his head, just like you!'

And Dan said, 'It's the fashion.'

The man shouted down, 'Can't you see I'm closed? Come back tomorrow!'

Walt said, 'I got a hundred dollars burnin' a hole in my pocket, and I wanna give it to you!'

Which got the man's attention. '*What?*' he said.

'I got a hundred dollars, and I wanna give it to you.'

The man stopped looking angry, and started looking confused. 'Why do you want to give me a hundred dollars?'

'I want information,' Walt told him.

'Information about what?'

'I'll tell you soon as you open this door.'

The man thought about that for a moment, then he said, 'I ain't opening the door in the middle of the night till I see your money.'

So Walt reached into his pocket and – to the surprise of the storekeeper and Dan Harbin and Ned Grimes – produced a stack of bills.

'Hold that up, so I can see,' said the storekeeper.

Walt held it up so he could see.

'How do I know they're real?' asked the storekeeper.

'You'll know they're real soon as you get down here and open the door and look at 'em up close,' said Walt.

The man thought some more and said, 'What's the catch?'

And Walt said, 'There ain't no catch.'

The man chewed his lip, rubbed his bandaged head and said, 'I don't know. . . .'

So Walt shrugged and said, 'OK,' and shoved the bills back in his pocket, unhitched his horse and started to ride off towards the saloon.

'Hey!' yelled the storekeeper, 'Wait a minute! I didn't say I wouldn't open the door. I just need a moment to think about it.'

Walt stopped his horse and turned around in his saddle. 'Is it gonna be a short moment or a long

88

moment? I don't mind, but my horse minds, on account of he ain't eaten all day and—'

'All right, all right,' said the storekeeper 'I'll open up. You just wait there.'

His head disappeared from the window. They heard his footfalls as he came downstairs, then the door being unlocked. It swung open.

By this time, Walt had got down off his horse and was once more outside the door.

'Where's the hundred dollars?' asked the store-keeper.

Walt drove his fist deep into the man's gut. The man doubled over and made an *oof!* noise as all the air rushed out of him. Walt pushed him inside the store. While the others entered behind him and closed the door, he took out the poster with Lee's picture on it and held it in front of the man's face. 'You seen him?'

'Yeah,' gasped the man, in between trying to suck in air.

'He break your window?'

'Kinda.'

'What do you mean, "kinda"?'

'He and another fella. . . . Robbed my store. . . . Last night. . . . The fella in the poster was gonna shoot me. The other fella threw his gun at me. Hit me on the head as I fired. The bullet went through the damned window. Then the man who threw the gun slugged me – knocked me out cold.'

Walt didn't quite know what to make of that, but he wasn't about to let it worry him much. The important thing was, Lee had been here. 'Did you shoot him?'

'Who?'

Walt slapped the bent-over storekeeper across the back of the head. 'The man in the poster, who d'you think I mean?'

'No. I told you, the shot went wide. . . . It went through the window, I told you. And when I woke up again, they were both gone.'

Walt looked at the floor. 'Where was he standing?'

'About where you are.'

Walt said to Ned and Dan, 'You see any blood?'

They looked at the floor, but they couldn't see any stains.

Walt said to the storekeeper, 'Did you see any blood on this floor when you woke up? Have you cleaned up any blood?'

'No, I swear,' said the storekeeper.

'Do you live alone?' asked Walt.

'What?'

'*Do you live alone? Is there anybody upstairs?*'

'No. I mean – I live alone.'

Walt drew his gun and held it against the man's head.

'No!' yelled Dan Harbin. He knew he was an outlaw – or at least, he was pretty sure. He didn't know how many men he'd killed in his lifetime, but one thing he *did* know: he couldn't stand by while Walt Crane shot this storekeeper in cold blood.

Walt looked at Dan. But he kept the gun barrel against the storekeeper's head. 'One thing we oughta get straight, right from the start,' he said. 'When you ride with me, you never ever question my orders, or tell me "no". You got that?'

Dan noticed that Ned Grimes had edged away and had turned a little toward him, his hand on the butt of his revolver. He figured he had to agree. And once he'd agreed, he might still just be able to persuade Walt to let the storekeeper live. 'Yeah,' said Dan. 'I got it.'

'Good,' said Walt, a grin spreading across his face. 'I'm glad. I didn't want us to argue, what with you being the fella who saved my brother's life, and all.'

'Yeah,' said Dan, forcing himself to grin back. 'And since I'm the fella who saved your brother's life, maybe you could—'

He didn't finish what he was saying. He was interrupted by the noise of Walt's gun as he shot the storekeeper through the head.

CHAPTER ELEVEN

At the hacienda down in Sonora, Lee Crane said to Tom Jericho, 'I'm getting kinda restless, sitting around here. You wanna come with me?'

'Sure,' said Jericho. He figured that once he'd got Lee alone he might learn something. He was certain he wasn't going to learn anything while he rattled around inside the house.

According to Lee, this place had been the Crane gang's hideout – one of them, anyway – for nearly two years, but there wasn't a damn thing, so far as Jericho could see, that gave any indication of what Walt was intending to do. Lee had said he had no idea what was being planned, but maybe he was lying. Or maybe he *did* know something important, but didn't *know* he knew it. . . .

Lee shouted at Lopita, who was in the kitchen, 'We're going out for a ride, Lopita.'

And she said, 'How long you goin' to be? I'm

making dinner. I cook chicken.'

And Lee said, 'I dunno. Hour or two, maybe.'

'I wish I knew when your brother and his men were due back.'

'Yeah, me too.'

So Lee and Jericho went out back to the stables to saddle their horses.

A couple of minutes later, while Jericho was fixing the reins around his horse's muzzle, he saw movement out of the corner of his eye. He looked out into the sunlit courtyard that lay between the hacienda and the stable buildings. Lopita was out there, scattering food for the dozen or so chickens clucking around her feet.

She threw the food down and they all bent their heads and pecked at it. The moment she'd thrown down the last handful, her arm lashed out, swift as a rattler, and caught one of the chickens by the neck.

The creature flapped and squawked in alarm. She held it to her breasts and cooed to it like a mother to a babe, and the bird calmed down, lulled by the woman's soothing tones. She smiled.

And then she twisted its neck between her powerful hands, snapping the spine and tearing the head clean off.

The woman chuckled, tossed the head away, and disappeared into the cool of the house.

The chickens continued to peck at the scattered feed, while only a few yards away the torn-off head of their former companion lay in the sunshine, a trickle of blood seeping on to the packed-down earth of the courtyard.

'You ready?' asked Lee, climbing on to his horse.

'Almost,' said Jericho.

They rode south till they got to a high ridge.

When they got to the top, Lee pointed down into the next valley. 'Looks like we're gonna get a free show.'

'What you talkin' about?' asked Jericho.

'What do you see?'

Jericho shaded his eyes and looked down into the valley. He saw a huddle of adobe buildings, people walking around: men, women, children. He saw old people, young people; he saw mules, dogs. . . .

'It's a village,' he said. 'So?'

'Look over there.' Lee was pointing to where a cloud of dirt was rolling across the floor of the valley in the direction the village.

'Riders,' said Jericho. 'A lot of 'em. And wagons.'

Some of the villagers saw the approaching horsemen and raised the alarm. Immediately there was panic. The villagers disappeared into their houses and Jericho heard screams of terror wafting up to him from out of the valley.

Lee was laughing, rolling a cigarette. 'I sure wish I'd bought a telescope with me!'

'Who are they?' asked Jericho. 'Bandits?'

'The riders? Naw, they're not bandits. They're Mexican Army.'

As they watched, the approaching riders split into groups. Gunshots rang out, and plumes of smoke erupted from the windows of the houses. The soldiers fired back. Some of the menfolk, some womenfolk too, ran out into the open carrying rifles, and took up positions where they could fire at the army without putting their families at risk, but they were soon gunned down.

Within minutes it was all over. The sound of gunfire was replaced by a rising cry of anguish that rose up out of the valley, a hundred voices all crying in wordless pain and creating one continuous keening wail. And then, with all those who'd chosen to fight now dead, the remaining villagers were herded on to wagons.

Lee had about finished his second cigarette by now. He threw it over the ridge, down into the valley. 'Not much to see this time,' he said, sounding disappointed. 'Usually they put up more of a fight.' He spat into the dirt.

'Why are those people being forced out of their homes?' asked Jericho, watching the wagons, now full of people, roll out of the now empty village.

'That's a Yaquis village. You heard of the Yaquis people?'

'Some. But don't forget, I been in prison for ten years. We sometimes got news of what was happening out in the big wide world, but most of the time I had troubles enough of my own.'

Lee nodded. 'The Yaquis have lived in these parts

95

since Moses was a boy. But the Mexican Government is in cahoots with rich businessmen who want this land for mining and farming, and suchlike. But the Yaquis don't want to go. So what the government does is, they send the army to round 'em up, and then they send 'em all the way down to the Yucatan Peninsula, in the south of Mexico. 'Course, the Yaquis have started puttin' up a fight.'

Jericho said, 'So that's what the revolution is all about?'

Lee spat in the dirt again. 'The revolution ain't *all* about the Yaquis, but they're sure a part of it.' He turned his horse around. 'C'mon – I'll race you back to the hacienda.'

For various reasons, the Yaquis villagers, the delight Lopita had taken in tearing the head off the chicken, the danger and uncertainty of his situation, Jericho wasn't feeling hungry. But he forced himself. He figured there was no point in starving himself to death.

'Ain't this chicken the finest you ever tasted?' Lee asked, his mouth full.

Jericho thought of Lopita cooing at the bird just before she'd ripped its head off, and of her laugh of delight once she'd done it, and he remembered the chicken's head lying in the dirt. 'Yeah,' he said.

'She puts her own secret ingredient in it,' said Lee. 'That's what makes it taste so good. But she won't never tell us what it is.'

Jericho decided he didn't really want to know what the sick bitch put in it. The meat tasted sour to him. He took a slug of the Mexican wine they were drinking and said, 'Tell me more about the revolution.'

'What about it?'

'You said it wasn't only about the Yaquis people being forced off their land and taken way south. So what else is it about?'

Lee said, 'I ain't no expert, but a lot of it's to do with the president and how he lets huge areas of land to be bought up by businessmen who then do what the hell they want with it—'

'This is the farming and the mining you told me about?'

'Farming, mining, factories. . . . The village we saw being cleared today is part of land that's been bought by one of those businessmen. He'll bring in cheap European and Chinese labour – of course, Mexicans can work for him too, if they don't mind the low wages.'

Then Lopita came in and told them that Walt and his gang had arrived.

Jericho heard running, and a second later a tall, lean man burst into the room.

Lee saw him, cried, 'Walt!' and jumped up out of his chair. The brothers laughed and hugged, slapping each other on the back.

So that's what Walt Crane looks like, thought Jericho. He'd seen pictures of the man, but in the flesh he was different. The way he moved was somehow reptilian, and you could sense the danger.

Behind the two brothers, more men flooded into the room, mostly grinning like idiots, either because they were glad to see Lee, or – more likely, Jericho figured – because their boss was in a good mood.

Then Jericho felt like the world had somehow dropped away from under his feet.

Dan Harbin was standing in the doorway.

What the hell was *he* doing here?

CHAPTER TWELVE

Harbin stood in the doorway. Over the heads of the gang he saw a man seated at the far end of a massive dining table. The man looked familiar, but he couldn't say why. . . .

If the young fella now embracing Will Crane was Will's younger brother Lee, then maybe the seated man was the other prisoner whom Dan had helped escape from the train. That would explain why he looked familiar. But it didn't explain why, deep inside Dan's head, a warning voice seemed to be trying to make itself heard.

The hot Mexican sun had dropped beyond the western horizon, and the sky had turned from blue to black. Jericho stood in the courtyard behind the hacienda, smoking a cigar.

From inside the house came the sound of drunken revelry. The old Mexican woman had gone to bed after feeding the gang, so now it was all men together, getting drunk. After a while Jericho had felt the need to get outside and clear his head. He'd drunk a few whiskeys – it would have looked mighty strange if he hadn't – but he was worried in case he made a slip. If Walt or Lee or any of their gang suspected he was a spy, he was as good as dead.

Worse than dead.

They'd want to extract as much information from him as they could, and they wouldn't kill him till they were satisfied they knew everything.

He was about halfway down his cigar when he heard a footstep behind him. It was Dan Harbin. He wasn't wearing his hat and the bandage around his head looked very white in the darkness.

'Thought I saw you come out here,' Dan said, rolling a cigarette.

'How's the head?' asked Jericho.

Dan gave a wan smile. 'The wound's healing fine. It's just. . . .'

'Yeah?'

'I can't remember much.' He finished rolling his cigarette and struck a match on the wall of the hacienda.

As Dan held the flame to the cigarette, Jericho could see that the man's eyes were full of questions, dozens of them, all lining up to be asked.

Jericho said, 'What *do* you remember?'

'I remember waking up at the dentist's. Lee was there – and you, I reckon. I ain't sure. That part's a little hazy. . . .'

'We had to leave you with the dentist and his wife. Sorry about that.'

Dan grinned. 'That's OK, I would've done the same. . . . My memory really only gets clear after you left. But what's worrying me is, I can't remember anything from before I was shot.' Dan stared at Jericho. 'Can I trust you?'

'Sure,' said Jericho.

Dan's voice dropped to a whisper. 'I can remember growing up, just about. My ma, my pa, stuff from way back . . . but from being full-grown, I don't recall nothing.'

'Nothing at all?'

'It's like I've been asleep, and I've been dreaming. But as soon as I try to pin down one of the dreams, it slips away. . . . Guess you must think I'm loco.'

'No,' said Jericho. 'I don't. Do you think your memory will come back to you?'

Dan inhaled smoke and drew it in deep before blowing it up at the moon. 'I don't know. Sometimes I think my memories are getting clearer, and any moment I'm gonna remember everything I've done, both good and bad. Including stuff I maybe don't want to remember.'

'Like what?'

Dan's eyes searched Jericho's. 'We know each other, right? I guess that's why I wanted to talk to you, nobody else. We're – we're friends, right?'

'Sure we are,' said Jericho.

'We known each other a long time?'

'Years,' lied Jericho.

'We're outlaws,' said Dan. 'I know that, but. . . .'

'But what?'

'I've killed, haven't I?'

Jericho didn't know for sure, but he guessed the answer had to be yes. 'Yeah,' he replied.

'How many?'

'I don't know.'

Dan threw the butt of his cigarette on to the ground and trod it into the dirt with his boot heel. 'That many, huh? So many, you can't even count 'em. I wonder how many widows and orphans I've made.' He turned and went back into the hacienda.

Jericho watched him till he'd disappeared inside, wanting to say something. . . .

But what *could* he have said? *You're not an outlaw, and neither am I. You're an employee of the US Government, and I'm some fella fresh out of state prison, and we're supposed to be spying on Walt Crane and his gang, on account of somebody thinks they're about to do something real bad.* Something like that? Jericho was having trouble coping with the situation himself, so how could he expect Dan Harbin to cope with it, the way his mind was right now?

On the other hand, if Jericho didn't tell him anything, what if Dan started remembering things, and put both their lives in danger? What if he remembered that he and Jericho were working for the government, and blurted it out before he remembered that he was supposed to keep his mouth shut?

Jericho scratched at the stubble on his jaw. This was one hell of a fix. . . .

And what was he supposed to do with any information he discovered? He'd been told to write down what he'd learned on to one of the squares of cards he'd been given – like the calling cards that rich people had, except blank on both sides. Then he was supposed to roll the card into a tube, push the tube into the butt of a cigar, and drop the butt somewhere. He'd been told not to worry about whether the message would be found: it *would* be found, that was all he needed to know. . . .

The problem was, it was Dan Harbin who was supposed to have been the one doing the finding.

Jericho cussed and went back inside.

Walt and Lee and two other members of the gang were having a rowdy game of poker. A couple of others were arm wrestling, cheered on by the rest, who were betting on the result. Dan was in a corner, pouring himself a whiskey.

Jericho yawned. He was thinking it was about time he got some shuteye, when Walt leapt on to the table and said, 'Boys, you all know I've been planning something big. Well, it's past midnight, and I can tell you now that by the time midnight rolls around again, you're all going to be rich!'

Jericho opened his eyes.

He was lying on top of a bed in a room on the upper storey of the hacienda, fully dressed in case he had to move fast. So he'd taken off his boots and his hat and gunbelt, and that was all. Although his gunbelt was hanging from the bed post, his gun was under his pillow.

Something had woken him up.

The room was pretty much in darkness, except for a shaft of moonlight that was sneaking in through a gap in the shutters. Without moving, his eyes scanned as much of the room as he could see. His hand slid up underneath the pillow and closed around the butt of his six-shooter.

He heard the sound of a floorboard creaking, but it wasn't inside the room; it was outside in the hallway.

Jericho got up out of the bed, slowly and carefully so he didn't make the bed creak. Holding his breath, he padded over to the door and pressed his ear against it. Somebody was out there, moving in the direction of the stairs. They were being sneaky about it, so they wouldn't be heard.

Jericho waited till they'd reached the stairway, then he unlocked and opened the door and crept out.

There was a window at one end of the hallway, and the window and the hallway were in a direct line with the moon, so that its silver glare shone all the way down the length of the passage, making it almost bright as day. If anybody was to look into the hallway now, there'd be no shadows in which to hide. They'd see him clear as if it was noon: Tom Jericho, creeping around without his boots on, a revolver in his hand.

He got to the end of the hallway and peered around the corner of the wall, in case whoever he was following had heard him, and was waiting for him on the stairway. . . .

But the stairway was clear.

Jericho descended carefully, remembering that the seventh step up from the bottom creaked. He reached the ground floor, looked around. Nothing moved.

Then he heard something from the back of the hacienda. A scraping noise, like a hinge that hadn't been oiled awhile. He moved towards the back of the house, but hadn't gone more than five steps before a voice said, 'Don't move, or I'll shoot.'

CHAPTER THIRTEEN

Tom Jericho froze. Seconds ticked by. The voice didn't speak again. Jericho said, 'Well?'

The voice said, 'I didn't mean to kill him, Ma. . . .'

Jericho turned slowly. The voice belonged to Ned Grimes, Walt Crane's sidekick, or second-in-command, or whatever he was. He was dreaming.

'It wasn't my fault – he asked for it!' murmured Ned.

Jericho left him and continued to the back door of the hacienda.

It was unlocked. He swung the door open gently. The hinge gave a scraping noise. This was the noise he'd heard earlier. He paused, listening.

There was the sound of another door being opened, but it was from way over the other side of the courtyard, where the stable block was.

Jericho put his eye to the gap between the door and the frame and looked out into the moonlit

courtyard. He stared, unblinking, alert for movement. . . .

Then, in one of the stables, he saw the light of a
match flaring. The flare died down and was replaced
by a flickering yellow flame.

Whoever was out there had lit a candle.

Jericho opened the back door just enough for him
to slip though, out into the moonlight. Quickly and
silently he made for the shadows, then worked his
way from shadow to shadow till he reached the
stables.

There were no windows on the back walls of the
stable block, and no side doors at either end. If
Jericho was going to get inside, he'd have to do it
from one of the doors at the front.

There were three big double doors, one in the
middle and one at each end. The light he'd seen had
come from the door on the left. He chose the door
on the right.

The stables weren't locked, just bolted. Inside, the
stables were effectively one long room, separated
into stalls with wooden divisions about as high as a
horse's shoulder, and each stall fronted by its own
door.

Jericho could just about hear the sound of
someone moving around in there at the far end of
the building. He slid the bolt across, barely making a
noise, and peered around the edge of the door.

There was a glow coming from inside the furthest
stall. He sneaked inside, pulled the door shut behind

him and edged towards the other end of the building. It was a lot darker in here than it was outside, so he had to be careful where he put his feet. Mostly, the floor of the stables consisted of paving slabs covered with straw, and the straw rustled as he put his weight on it. That was bad enough, but somebody might have left a bucket or something lying around, so he moved slowly.

From the far stall came a sound like a wooden box lid being wrenched open.

In the stall alongside Jericho, a horse whinnied.

In the far stall, the noises stopped.

There was absolute silence for about five long seconds, then Jericho heard a sound that caused his blood to turn to ice: it was the sound of a revolver's hammer being cocked.

The door of each stall came up to the horse's chest, but it didn't reach all the way down to the floor. Between the bottom of the door and the floor was a gap of about eighteen inches. Jericho got down on his hands and knees and crawled through the gap. The horse inside the stall began to snort in agitation as Jericho edged past its flank to the back of the stall.

Meanwhile the candle was moving, the shadows inside the stable shifting crazily as whoever was in the far stall picked it up and came to investigate the cause of the horse's distress. The other horses had been disturbed now, and had also started kicking up a ruckus.

'Who's there?' said the voice. It was Walt Crane's voice. 'Whoever it is, you better come out now, otherwise I'll get mad as hell. And when I'm mad as hell, there's no telling what I might do. Why, one time I skinned a fella—' He broke off, interrupted by a noise that pierced the night, cutting through the snorting and whinnying of the horses.

Outside in the courtyard, a coyote was howling at the moon.

'Why, I'll be a son of a bitch!' swore Walt. 'Goddamn coyote got the infernal cheek to come down off the hills and down to the goddamn house! Why, he'd sleep in my bed if I let him!'

Walt backed up, put down the candle he'd been holding, and opened the door he'd entered through earlier, all the time cussing to himself. 'Goddamn son of a bitch! I'm gonna get you this time!'

Listening, Jericho figured this must be some kind of long-standing feud. Or at least, that's what Walt seemed to think it was. What the coyote thought was another matter.

Jericho thought Walt was going to shoot the coyote, but as long seconds stretched out, there was no gunshot. Instead, Jericho heard Walt say, 'Come on, you mean-eyed son of a bitch! Come on!'

Jericho couldn't help himself. He had to take a look. He crept over to the half-open doorway and looked out into the courtyard.

The square of the courtyard was a pool of moonlight, and on it two wild, untameable creatures – one with two legs, the other with four – circled each other.

The coyote circled Walt, who'd put his gun away and now had a knife in his hand and, while the coyote growled from somewhere deep inside its chest, Walt crooned to it, saying, 'Come on. . . . That's right, you dirty bastard, come and get me. . . .'

The coyote sprang into the air, teeth bared. Its front paws hit Walt in the chest and he fell backwards into the dirt. There came a growling noise, but Jericho, watching, couldn't be sure if it came from the coyote or from Walt, or both. Walt's left hand had grabbed a fistful of the animal's fur and was trying to push its head away from him, the coyote's teeth a bare inch from Walt's neck. Then the coyote gave a yelp of pain and there was blood spurting on to Walt and on to the moonlit courtyard. The knife had pierced the coyote's heart. The animal went limp, and collapsed on top of him.

Walt just lay there in the dirt with the dead coyote on his chest, its blood running on to his face and arms. He was breathing heavily, exhausted. For several seconds he lay there, and then a sound like choking came up from his throat.

That's what Jericho thought he was doing at first – choking. But then as the choking got louder, he realized that what Walt was doing wasn't choking: he was laughing.

Jericho remembered how he'd seen the old Mexican woman tear the head off the chicken earlier that day, and it seemed to him that the people around here just loved killing. And it didn't seem to matter much what they killed: so long as they killed, they were happy.

Walt Crane stopped laughing and rolled out from under the animal.

Jericho backed away from the door, but instead of returning to the stall in which he'd been hiding, he went into the stall that Walt had been in. There was no horse in this stall. The candle wasn't in here now – Walt had carried it out to the door – and all Jericho could tell in the darkness was that Walt had opened some boxes in there. But whatever the boxes contained, he couldn't say.

Jericho wasn't wearing his holster, so he pushed his gun into his jeans belt. He climbed up on to the wooden partition that separated this stall from the next. Balancing on top of it, Jericho grabbed hold of a roof beam and hauled himself up.

He'd laid himself flat on the beam just as Walt came back into the stables, wiping his bloodied hands on his jeans. Walt picked up the candle, by now melted down to little more than a stub, and carried it into the stall.

Now Jericho could see the boxes clearly. And – thanks to Walt having prised the lids off and propped them against the wall – he could see inside them.

The boxes were coffin-sized, but they didn't contain bodies. One contained rifles and ammunition. The other contained clothes of some kind, together with a smaller box with DYNAMITE stencilled in big, bold, angry letters down the side.

Jericho watched from above as Walt placed the candle on top of the partition and used his knife – still stained with the coyote's blood – to open the box containing the explosives.

Once Walt had worked the nails loose and lifted the lid, Jericho saw that, sure enough, it contained sticks of dynamite. Enough to. . . .

What?

Wreck every railroad line between here and Tucson?

Blast open every bank safe in Sonora?

Blow an entire town to kingdom come?

Walt closed the box and replaced the lids on the two larger boxes. Then he grabbed armfuls of straw and spread it over them. Not to hide them, just to make the boxes look like they weren't anything worth bothering with. Then he picked up the candle and left the stables, bolting the door behind him.

Jericho waited a couple of minutes, giving Walt time to get back to the house, then lowered himself down off the roof beam. He made his way to the other end of the stables, to the door he'd entered through.

Using the shadows as before, he worked his way around the periphery of the courtyard to the back door of the hacienda.

With luck, Walt would have gone to bed and wouldn't hear him re-enter the house.

Jericho turned the handle and tried to open the door.

It was locked.

CHAPTER FOURTEEN

The hacienda was as impregnable as a fortress. Jericho went around the side and sat against the wall. Above him the sky lightened. He was dozing with his head in his arms when he was woken up by the sound of the back door opening.

The sun was still low. Jericho figured it was about six o'clock, something like that. He peered around the wall and there was Lopita standing in the courtyard, staring down at the dead coyote and talking to herself in Spanish. Eventually she quit staring and talking and went back inside the house, leaving the back door open.

Jericho followed her inside.

He could hear her somewhere close, moving stuff around, still muttering something. Pulling his tobacco and papers out of his vest pocket, he rolled a cigarette and lit it. When Lopita reappeared, he was leaning against the door, smoking.

She hadn't expected to see anybody. When she saw him she said, 'Oh!' and jumped a little, then said something in Spanish that Jericho didn't under-stand, but he guessed it was one of the more obscure cuss words.

'Hi Lopita,' he said, grinning.

She looked at him curiously. 'I didn't hear you.'

'I ain't got my boots on.'

The woman looked at his feet, saw he was wearing only socks, and shrugged.

He nodded at the dead coyote in the courtyard. 'That what we're having for breakfast?'

Lopita grunted, in no mood for humour. She'd put on a pair of thick leather gloves, and now she went back over to the dead coyote, grabbed it by the back legs, and started hauling it out of the courtyard.

That is one strong old woman, thought Jericho. She can twist a chicken's head clean off, and she can drag a dead coyote's carcass around all on her own.

'You need help with that?' he asked her for chivalry's sake, though he knew she didn't need any help. Lopita had probably never needed help with anything. She glared at Jericho for an instant, spat on to the packed-down earth of the courtyard and carried on hauling the carcass.

Jericho wondered if the woman had ever loved, or been loved. Had she ever cried? Had she ever laughed for any other reason than she'd just killed a living creature? How did people like Lopita get to be like that? He didn't know, and wasn't prepared to spend much time pondering the question. He smoked the rest of his cigarette and threw the butt out into the courtyard. It fell in the dark red stain where the coyote had bled out. The blood couldn't have completely dried, because the glowing butt sizzled when it landed.

Jericho made his way back upstairs. Having drunk themselves stupid the night before, the gang was still asleep. He returned to his room and lay on the bed.

With luck he'd be able to get a couple of hours' shuteye before whatever Walt Crane had planned for today started happening.

Dan Harbin was dreaming.

He was dreaming that he was a lawman, and he'd just hanged a man from a gallows. But when he looked up at the face of the man who'd been hanged, he saw that the face was his own, the eyes bulging out of the purple face, and the swollen tongue sticking out from a mouth that wasn't big enough to hold it anymore.

And when he turned around he saw that his ma and pa were behind him, his ma crying, and his pa saying, 'You've killed our boy.'

And Dan shouted, '*I'm a lawman! It's my job! I'm a lawman! I'm a lawman!*' He shouted louder and louder, till the words seemed to echo inside his own skull. . . .

He woke up. His eyes snapped open and his hand

116

went to his gun. It wasn't there. . . .

Then he remembered that after he'd come upstairs to one of the bedrooms, he'd taken off his gunbelt and laid it on the floor on the side of the bed away from the door. Sunlight was seeping in through the cracks in the shutters. In the half light he reached over the edge of the bed and found his gun.

With the weight of the revolver in his hand he felt a little better.

Had he cried the words *I'm a lawman!* out loud? If he had, and somebody had heard him, he could quickly wind up dead.

If they find out I'm a lawman, they'll kill me.

But I'm not a lawman – I'm an outlaw. . . .

His mind full of confusion, Dan lay back on the bed. Sweat was breaking out on his forehead, soaking into the bandage wrapped around his skull.

Am I an outlaw, or a lawman?

He didn't know what the hell he was.

If he was a lawman, what the hell was he doing down here in Sonora with the Crane Gang?

A voice from somewhere beyond the foot of the bed drawled, 'Something bothered me the moment I set eyes on you, but I didn't figure out what it was till a little while ago.'

Dan jerked up in bed, aiming his revolver in the direction of the voice.

The man was seated on a cane chair, leaning back against the wall. A shaft of pinkish early morning light illuminated one side of his face.

Dan could see it was Hector Mead, one of the oldest members of the gang. He was a thin, pinched-faced man with a pencil moustache and a little triangle of goatee beard that made him look like one of the old-time Mississippi gamblers.

'You know how it is, when you've had a few drinks, and something occurs to you? Like the booze has loosened something in your brain? Well, it was in the small hours that I realized what it was about you that was bothering me. I've seen you before.'

'That a fact?' said Dan.

'It's a fact,' said Hector. 'But even then, I couldn't place you. Not till a couple of more drinks later. Then I had it: you're a Texas Ranger.'

Dan kept the revolver pointed directly at Hector's forehead. 'I am?'

'At least you were eight years ago, when you shot me.'

'I shot you?'

'You don't recall? I'm offended. Me and my gang – I had my own gang back then – we'd just finished robbing a bank. We didn't know we had Texas Rangers on our trail. We were ambushed. My gang was all killed, but you shot me in the left shoulder. My luck was in. I fell off a cliff into a river, and the water swept me away. You never did catch up with me.'

'Eight years is a long time,' said Dan. 'You could be mistaken.'

Hector shook his head. 'I never forget a face. It

was you shot me – and now I'd like to return the favour.'

Dan clicked back the hammer on his six-gun. 'Maybe I'd better shoot you again,' he said. 'And this time, I ain't gonna shoot you in the shoulder.'

Hector grinned. 'You could try that, but I better tell you – when I came in here a few minutes ago, when you were still sleepin', I took the bullets out of your gun. Then I sat down and watched you, to make sure you were who I thought you were. Then you started cryin' out in your sleep about how you were a lawman, and that kinda settled any doubt that might have still been lingerin' in my head.' He reached down to his gunbelt and drew his revolver.

Dan squeezed the trigger on his gun, but the hammer clicked uselessly on an empty chamber.

Hector's grin got broader. 'You thought I was bluffin', didn't you?' He aimed his revolver square in the middle of Dan's chest. 'My turn,' he said.

Dan saw Hector's finger tense as he prepared to fire. 'Don't you want to know what I'm doing here?' he asked.

Hector's finger relaxed. 'So tell me. I'm curious. What *are* you doin' here?'

'I ain't a Texas Ranger no more,' said Dan, not knowing if that was true or not. 'I killed a man in an argument. I had to go on the run, so I became an outlaw.' Dan was making this up – or at least, he *hoped* he was making it up.

Hector shrugged. 'Makes no difference to me if

you're still a ranger or not. Fact is, eight years ago, you and your ranger friends killed my gang, and *you personally* shot me. That's all I care about.' He squeezed the trigger.

Dan rolled sideways off the bed as Hector fired. The bullet hit the wall, missing Dan's head by an inch. He crashed on to the ground, reaching down towards his ankle.

A second bullet hit the metal bed frame and ricocheted off. Dan grabbed the tiny derringer strapped to his shin. Pulling it free of its holster, he raised the gun and shot Hector just as he was about to fire for a third time.

The bullet hit Hector in the left eye and burrowed deep into his brain, not stopping till it struck the back of his skull.

Hector's body went into spasm for a moment, but then he slumped back in his chair, stone dead.

A couple of seconds later, the hallway outside was full of people.

Dan figured he had about half a second to come up with a damn good story.

The gang burst in. In the lead was Ned Grimes. He looked down at Hector Mead, who still had a smoking six-gun in his hand, and then looked at Dan Harbin, sitting up behind the bed, holding his derringer. 'What the hell happened?' he asked.

'That damned fool!' yelled Dan. 'He said I stole a ruby ring off him. I didn't even know he *had* a ruby ring.'

Ned looked down at Hector's hands, and the dead man certainly wasn't wearing any ruby ring now.

Behind Ned, one of the gang said, 'Hector was always complainin', and causin' trouble about somethin'.'

A couple of the others agreed. 'He threatened to cut my throat once,' said one, 'on account of he said I'd insulted his home state.'

'What *was* his home state?'

'Damned if I know. Wyoming . . . Montana maybe. . . . Somewhere up there.'

Ned looked at Dan and said, 'Lucky for you, Hector was an ornery cuss. I don't suppose anybody will miss him much – though I guess Walt'll be a mite peeved. It means we'll be a man down.' He heaved a sigh and scratched his head. 'Never mind – guess it can't be helped. You better come downstairs, Lopita's making breakfast. We got a big day ahead.'

CHAPTER FIFTEEN

When Walt heard that Dan had shot Hector, he said, 'Guess Dan's saved me the trouble of shooting Hector myself. He was one contrary son of a bitch. Always belly-achin' about something. I guess someone better take him out into the desert before he starts to stink the place out.'

'I'll take care of it,' said Ned.

'OK,' said Walt. 'But get Dan to help you. He had all the fun of shooting the bastard – it's only right he helps get rid of him.'

'You want us to bury him?'

'No, just dump him somewhere he won't be seen. The coyotes and the vultures will finish him off. But not now. I gotta talk to the men first. Get 'em all down here.'

Some of Walt's men had already brought the coffin-sized boxes in from the stables, and now the boxes lay in the centre of the big downstairs room, their lids still on. When all the men were gathered around him, Walt took out his knife and prised the boxes open. He hefted out one of the rifles. 'Old army rifles,' he said. He threw it to one of his men. 'That's what we're gonna use tonight.'

They all wondered *Use to do what?* but they kept their mouths shut.

Then he pulled out the clothes that had been bundled up in the other box, and dumped them on the floor. They were the kind of clothes they'd all seen Mexican workers wearing. Baggy, pale-coloured shirts and pants, and sweat-stained, misshapen sombreros.

Walt reached into the box again, this time pulling out bandoleers full of ammunition to wear across their chests. 'There's everything you'll need to look like one of them Yaquis revolutionaries who have been causing trouble for the mine owners down here,' he said. 'Everything except boots – you can wear your own.'

Bob Younger piped up, 'But some of us don't look like Yaquis. They're dark, and they got black hair.' Bob Younger was pale, with hair yellow as corn.

'I thought of that,' said Walt. 'There's stuff you can put on your faces and hair that'll make you look like a real Mex.'

Somebody else had spotted the box marked DYNA-MITE. 'What you gonna do with the dynamite, Walt?'

'You let me worry about that, Dex. Now, I figure you know about as much as you need to know for now. We leave at six o'clock. You're gonna be fed and rested, and look like Yaquis. And if I see anybody drinking liquor between now and then, I'll tell Lopita to slit his throat.'

Dex said, 'Does that include beer?'

Walt stared Dex in the eye. 'You want to take that risk, Dex?'

Dex blinked first.

'Better stick to coffee,' said Walt, grinning.

'Yeah,' said Dex, grinning back, but his voice caught as he said it.

When Walt had done with them, Dan Harbin went out into the courtyard. He'd been told how Walt had killed a coyote out there with a knife in the early hours of the morning. He smoked a cigarette, looking at the patch of dried blood on the baked earth, and the drag marks where it had been hauled away, and he thought about how easy it was to kill: coyote or a man, you could kill either, easy as blinking. A knife, or a bullet, or one of a hundred other means, it didn't matter. In an instant, all the dreams and hopes and all the good and bad that made a person were gone, and once you'd separated the soul from the body you couldn't put it back again, not ever.

He was a lawman, he was pretty sure of that now. But if that was so, what the hell was he doing here, with these son of a bitch outlaws?

He was spying on them.

That had to be it. He could think of no other

explanation. He must've been spying on them, pretending to be one of them, when he'd been shot in the head.

That would explain it.

But what about Jericho? Dan had the feeling that Tom Jericho was wanting to tell him something, but never quite came out with it – he could see it in his eyes, the way he moved.

Was Jericho a lawman too?

And if Jericho was a lawman, did that mean Lee Crane was also a lawman? Was that possible? Dan had helped both Jericho and Lee escape – or so he'd been told. And both Jericho and Lee had taken him to the dentist's to get his head patched up.

Could Lee Crane, brother of Walt Crane, really be on the side of the law?

Dan couldn't see how that was possible.

Just when he'd got himself about as confused as ever, a new memory came rushing back:

He and another man, on horseback. Dan had a knife; the other man had a gun. The other man was wearing a sheriff's badge. Dan's blade found the man's throat, while the sheriff's bullet carved a groove in Dan's head. . . .

Dan felt sick.

He'd killed a sheriff.

Maybe he'd been a Texas Ranger years ago, like Hector Mead had said, but since then he must have turned bad.

He *was* an outlaw after all. . . .

*

125

Six o'clock. The stars were out again. Somewhere a coyote was howling. Jericho remembered hearing once that coyotes didn't run in packs, like wolves, but in pairs. He wondered if this coyote was howling for the one that Walt had killed the previous night. The cry sounded pitiful enough.

They rode south and to the east, and after an hour or so the land became more fertile. They passed through a valley criss-crossed with irrigation ditches, then up over a hill and down again. Ahead of them a few miles distant was a city, all spread out under the big yellow Mexican moon.

Jericho angled his horse over to Dan Harbin's, and when nobody else was in earshot, said, 'How you feelin'?'

Dan said, 'About as good as a fella can be after he's shot a man.'

'I figure a lot of fellas around here would feel real good after they'd shot a man.'

'Well, I ain't one of them,' said Dan.

'Me neither,' said Jericho. 'You remembered any-thing more?'

'What?'

'You remembered anything more?'

Jericho thought Dan looked like he wanted to say something, but couldn't quite let himself say it.

'No,' Dan said.

'OK,' said Jericho.

They rode the rest of the way without talking again.

They entered the city of Hermosilla, Sonora's state capital, just before nine o'clock, and made their way around the outskirts till they reached the gates of a big old Spanish-style *casa*. Part of the roof had caved in, and it looked like nobody had lived there for years.

Ned Grimes got off his horse and dug around in his pockets.

Walt said, 'Don't tell me you've lost the key, Ned. I only gave it you this morning.'

'I got it, I got it!' Ned was starting to panic. But then he found the key and held it up. 'I told you I got it!'

'Congratulations,' said Walt. 'Now could you open the damn gates, afore somebody sees us?'

Ned unlocked the gates and swung them open.

The gang followed Walt through the gateway and rode around to the back of the *casa*, where a close-planted line of trees separated the *casa*'s grounds from the adjacent ptoperty.

Walt said, 'You men wait here and keep quiet. I'm gonna go play with this here dynamite.' He patted one of his saddle-bags.

By now Ned had closed the gates and had caught up with the rest of them behind the *casa*. Walt said to him, 'Keep the men here till you get the signal. Till then, make sure everybody stays quiet and out of sight. And nobody smoke. They'll see the glow of the cigarettes.'

Jericho wanted to say *Who will*, but he kept his mouth shut, and so did everybody else.

Walt held his hand out to Ned and Ned gave him the keys to the gates. 'I'll push it back under the gates once I've locked them again from the outside.'

Ned nodded, and Walt Crane rode off, leaving the gang sitting on their horses next to the line of trees.

The trees grew close enough to each other for their branches to weave together. Some kind of scrub grew up between them, and ivy coiled around the trunks. Through the scrub and the ivy and the inter-leaving branches, Jericho could see lights. As his eyes became used to the darkness he found he could see a mansion – bigger and newer and whiter than the house behind him. It looked like one of those Dixie plantation houses, with its columns, and the steps leading up to the main entrance.

Jericho could see carriages arriving, and men and women dressed in their best finery getting out of the carriages and walking arm-in-arm up the steps of the mansion, and disappearing inside.

The rest of the gang were watching just like he was, and in dead silence. Even the horses seemed to sense they had to keep quiet. Apart from the occasional snort or shuffling of hoofs, they barely made a sound.

With a sick feeling rising in his gut, Jericho realized what it was they were expected to do.

Dan Harbin didn't know it, but he realized what the

gang was meant to do at the exact same instant as Jericho.

They were meant to kill everybody in the mansion.

CHAPTER SIXTEEN

More people were arriving at the mansion. Another gentleman and lady had stepped down from a carriage and were climbing the steps to the entrance.

Between the mansion and the trees behind which the gang was hiding, was a square of lush green lawn, a couple of hundred feet along each side, with a circular flower bed in the middle of it. Jericho wondered how much it cost to grow and tend a lawn and flower bed like that out here in the Mexican heat.

The sound of a lilting waltz wafted across to them.

There wasn't any way he was going to ride across that lawn, and start shooting all those gentlemen and ladies. But how was he going to stop the rest of the gang? Besides Dan Harbin, Ned Grimes and Lee Crane, there were nine others, all of whom would kill him as soon as spit.

He glanced over to Harbin, and Jericho could see by the look on his face that he was thinking the very same thoughts. Jericho edged his horse over to Dan and whispered, 'Have you remembered you're really a lawman yet? Because if you *are* gonna remember, this would be a real good time.'

Dan stared at him, like this was some kind of trick. 'What? I don't . . . I. . . .'

'You're just *making believe* you're an outlaw,' said Jericho. 'So am I. We're both working for the US Government.'

Sweat had broken out all over Dan's face. He wiped the sweat away with his sleeve, and nodded. 'OK,' he mouthed, and Jericho thought he looked relieved.

'There are a lot more of them than there are of us,' said Jericho. 'We're gonna have to do some fancy shootin'.'

Dan nodded again. Then his eyes clouded a little. 'What about Lee? Is he with us, or against us?'

Jericho wondered for a moment if Dan was crazy, asking that. But then he figured, maybe from Dan's point of view it was a reasonable enough question. 'He's against us,' he said.

And then the whole night became bright as day as a big orange ball of flame rose into the sky on the other side of the mansion, and the earth shook, and the roar of the explosion rolled across the lawn towards them.

The sudden brightness and noise scared the horses. They reared up, and it was all the gang could do to stay on their mounts.

131

'There's our signal!' yelled Ned Grimes. 'Come on, boys! The time's come to earn your pay!' He led the charge, kicking his horse savagely in the flank and sending it galloping through the scrub between the trees.

As he burst through on to the lawn, the gang whooped and followed him. Not a single one of them seemed to be giving a thought to the fact that they were going to be slaughtering innocent folks.

'They're gonna kill all them people,' said Dan.

'Unless you want to ask 'em to turn around,' Jericho said, 'we're gonna have to shoot 'em in the back.'

'I don't believe I ever shot a man in the back before,' said Dan.

'Well, I know for certain I ain't,' said Jericho. 'It kinda goes against the grain, but if we're gonna save all them innocent people, that's what we're gonna have to do.'

They both raised their rifles and fired.

The gang had just about reached the flower bed, which was roughly the halfway point between the trees and the mansion. Two of the gang fell from their horses as Jericho and Dan Harbin's bullets found their intended targets.

They fired again, but this time only one rider fell, and by now some of the gang had figured they were being fired on from behind. They slowed up and turned in their saddles to see where the shooting was coming from, and a moment later Jericho saw plumes of smoke erupt from their rifles as they returned fire.

One of the gang's bullets hit a tree. Another whizzed past Jericho's head. Next to him, Dan aimed and fired, and the fella who'd just shot at Jericho fell from his horse.

Meanwhile, Ned Grimes and the four or five other riders had reached the steps of the mansion. They rode up the steps, Grimes shooting a man standing in the entrance. . . .

'C'mon, boys!' yelled Grimes, as they rode into the entrance hall.

The floor of the entrance hall was laid out with marble tiles, and his horse's iron-shod hoofs couldn't get much of a grip. So he reined in his horse to a trot and continued firing at just about anybody he could see – the more important they looked, the better.

Ned was the only one of the gang, including Walt's brother Lee, who had any idea what this massacre was all about.

A while back, Walt had met up with some rich Mexican politician who had his fingers in a lot of pies – mining, whatever. This politician had done deals with Walt before, though Ned didn't know any details about that. And the Mexican had told Walt that he'd been having trouble with the Yaquis revolutionaries who'd been disrupting mining and so forth.

The Mexican wanted to get tough on the revolutionaries, but some of the politicians in the Mexican

Government weren't willing to do whatever it took. It just so happened that some of these people were his political rivals. So he figured he could kill two or more birds with one stone by hiring Walt and his gang to dress up as Yaquis and raid the big political get-together that was going on tonight. He wasn't going to be there, but a lot of those rivals of his would be.

Another bonus was that the United States Consul and his wife would be at the get-together, too. The US Government disapproved of the treatment of the Yaquis, but no doubt that attitude would change once they heard their consul and his wife had been slaughtered in cold blood by 'Yaquis revolutionaries'.

So Walt would raid the party, kill a lot of the polit-ical rivals, the Yaquis would be blamed, and the crooked politician could use the situation to per-suade the rest of the government to wipe the Yaquis and all other revolutionaries off the face of the earth. Which meant they wouldn't be able to disrupt his damn mines anymore.

And all, hopefully, without the condemnation – or intervention – of the United States.

In return, Walt and his gang would earn them-selves a wagonload of silver and be able to live like kings for the rest of their lives.

Inside the mansion, Ned Grimes walked his horse into the ballroom, reloading his rifle and shooting as he went. The ladies and gentlemen were huddled against the walls. The women – painted-up and

dressed in satin and silk and taffeta – were screaming, and the men were ashen-faced, trying to protect
them. They hadn't expected any kind of threat
tonight, so only the occasional one had a pistol. Even
those who *had* brought firearms with them had only
fancy little pocket guns with them: one- or two-shot
mostly, small calibre, difficult to aim and barely more
lethal than a child's catapult over a distance of more
than a few feet.

Out of the corner of his eye, Ned Grimes saw one
of the fine gentlemen – fifty, sixty years old, distin-
guished-looking with a mane of white hair – pull one
of the fancy little guns out of his jacket and aim it at
him. The gun made a cracking noise, and Ned felt
the bullet graze his shoulder.

'You son of a bitch!' yelled Ned, forgetting he
wasn't supposed to speak English, and shot the man
in the middle of his frilly white shirt.

The rifle bullet went clean through the man and
he toppled to the ground, stone dead. Ned's bullet,
after going clean through the man, had buried itself
in the chest of a young *señorita*, now looking down
with her mouth wide open at the bloody hole that
had suddenly opened up between her breasts. She
looked up and her eyes met Ned's, then she too collapsed to the floor, dead.

Ned laughed, pleased with himself. *Two corpses with
one bullet!*

Behind him, Lee said, 'Where're the others?'

Ned turned. 'What you talking about?'

135

'The rest of the gang.'

Looking past him, Ned could only count four other members of Walt's gang, killing people as they had been instructed.

They were all supposed to be in here, shooting. So where the hell were the rest?

Ned also saw that some of the people, having recovered from the shock of the explosion and the shock of finding themselves being shot at, had burst open some of the French windows and were running out into the night.

He swore. This wasn't supposed to happen. Hardly anybody was supposed to get out of the mansion alive. One or two maybe, so they could tell everybody they'd been attacked by the Yaquis, but most of the guests were supposed to wind up dead. That's what the gang was being paid for.

And it was taking far too long, Ned realized. If all of the gang had ridden in here and started shooting, they way they'd been told, they'd have just about finished by now. 'Where the hell are those bastards?' Ned yelled.

He dug his spurs into his horse's flank, intending to gallop out of the ballroom, through the entrance hall and down the steps of the mansion. The horse got as far as the entrance hall, but as soon as its hoofs hit the marble floor, its legs slid from under it and the animal crashed on to its side, pinning Ned's leg beneath it.

CHAPTER SEVENTEEN

After leaving his gang by the trees, Walt Crane had ridden his horse back out on to the road, remembering to push the key back under the gates once he'd locked them again.

He mounted his horse, but before he set off he consulted the hand-drawn map Perez had given him. It showed where the cannery was that Perez wanted Walt to blow up. The cannery was owned by another of Perez's political rivals, a man who'd be at the mansion tonight.

Walt had suggested causing a distraction by dynamiting somewhere close by, which was intended to draw away the guards who would undoubtedly be posted so that the fine ladies and gentlemen could dance in safety, and Perez had suggested blowing up the cannery. Why not? If Walt was going to blow something up tonight anyway, why not blow up a factory belonging to one of Perez's rivals?

So Walt, after folding the map and tucking it under his 'Yaquis' shirt, rode off in the direction of the cannery.

There were guards there too, but that didn't bother Walt much. He wasn't going to even try getting through the gates. Adjacent to the cannery, right behind it, was a church and the church had a bell tower.

It was evening, the main door of the church was locked, but there was a back door, and this wasn't.

With the saddle-bags containing the dynamite slung over one shoulder, and a coil of rope slung over the other, he went inside the church and found himself in a small room which looked like some kind of kitchen.

He heard movement from an adjacent room. He went through and found a priest sitting at a desk, writing something. The priest looked up. The man was getting old, but was still young enough and big enough to be a threat. He said something in Spanish and began to rise, but before he was fully upright, Walt pistol-whipped him across the head and the priest fell back into the chair, out cold, blood leeching out from a cut under his greying hair.

Walt went into the church, found the door to the bell tower, and climbed. He was fit and fast, and it didn't take him more than a couple of minutes to get to the top.

From the bell tower he had a view of the roof of

the cannery about sixty feet below and thirty feet away horizontally.

Further off, about a quarter of a mile distant, was the mansion in which the dance was taking place. Walt could just about make out the trees beyond, behind which he'd left his gang waiting.

Leaving the sticks of dynamite in the saddle-bags, Walt fixed the fuse and tied one end of the rope to the broad strip of leather that connected the two bags. Then he climbed out of the bell tower and on to the ledge.

The fuse was long with a ten-minute delay. Once it had landed on the roof, nobody would see it. It was possible that somebody might hear the thump it made as it landed, but the cannery was empty apart from the guards – who'd probably be outside, not in. Usually the factory was a round-the-clock operation, but the workers had been given the night off, so that the guests at the nearby mansion wouldn't be disturbed by the noise of the canning machines.

Walt lit the fuse and swung the bags a few times, allowing the rope to lengthen each time he swung it, to get as much momentum as he could. Then on the seventh or eighth swing he let it go, and the bags went arcing off into the night, landing with a thud on the roof of the cannery.

He had ten minutes to get to safety. There was enough dynamite in the saddle-bags to destroy the factory and the church, and everything else within a 300-yard radius.

He charged down the spiral staircase, then retraced his steps through the church.

'*Parar!*'

As Walt passed through the tiny office, the priest was pushing himself up on to his feet and telling him to stop.

'Ain't got time to talk, Padre,' said Walt. But a second later the priest had grabbed him by the arm and had hauled him back into the room. The old man was strong. He pinned Walt up against the wall and started yelling at him in Spanish. Walt knew some Spanish, but this was too fast and too thickly-accented for him to understand.

'Padre,' said Walt, 'if you don't let go of me, I'm gonna have to plug ya. I ain't got time to mess around.'

But the priest wasn't going to let go any time soon. He just clung on to Walt, using his substantial weight to pin him against the wall, all the time mouthing words that Walt couldn't comprehend.

'Sorry to have to do this,' said Walt, pulling his gun. 'But then again, you were gonna get blown to kingdom come in a little while anyway, so I guess it don't really matter much. . . .'

He fired the gun into the padre's belly. The light dimmed in the priest's eyes, but his hands still gripped Walt's shoulders, and when the priest toppled to the floor, Walt fell with him. As he fell, Walt's head crashed into the corner of the writing desk, knocking him out cold.

When he regained consciousness, Walt could smell varnish. He opened his eyes. The varnish had been used to shine the wooden floor on which he was lying.

Where the hell was he?

He pushed himself up on to his knees, and saw the priest lying next to him, dead. Then he remembered the dynamite.

It had a ten-minute fuse, but Walt had no idea how much time had passed while he'd been lying, out cold, on the floor. For all he knew, the whole church could be blown to fragments any moment, with him inside.

He ran out of the church, untied his horse and threw himself on to its back. He'd been urging the horse on at full gallop for almost a minute when the sky lit up behind him and he felt the heat of the explosion on his back.

The roar and the force of it surged over him like a tide. The horse panicked, bucking, and the next thing he knew Walt was lying in a ditch at the side of the road, looking up at a sky full of angry orange flame.

When Walt hauled himself out of the ditch, the horse was nowhere to be seen. He checked himself for injuries, but apart from a bruised ass, singed hair and a ringing in his ears, he was OK.

He started to walk back to the ruined *casa* where he'd left his men. The ringing in his ears subsided, and he heard shooting.

The massacre had begun.

He smiled.

Soon he was going to be rich.

Ned Grimes lay on the floor of the entrance hall, his leg still pinned beneath his fallen horse. The animal squirmed, kicked and got itself to its feet, shakily made its way across the tiles, and ran out into the night.

Ned tried to get up, but couldn't: his leg was broken.

He looked around for help, but there wasn't any. Lee Crane had gone, and those other members of the gang who had followed Ned into the mansion were now lying dead, small-calibre bullets in their heads.

If the rest of the gang had stormed the mansion as they had been ordered, the killing would have been done quickly; nobody would have had time to retaliate.

What had gone wrong?

All the fine ladies and gentlemen were gathering around him. A woman in a pink silk dress with somebody's blood all down the front of it leaned over him, screamed at him in Spanish and spat in his face.

Ned drew his gun and aimed it at her, but strong hands grabbed his arm and tore the pistol from his fist.

Then an elderly gentleman with a lean, hook-nosed face like a medieval Spanish grandee, pulled

142

an ornamental sword from off the wall and advanced on Ned. Ned started to laugh.

So this is how it's gonna end, he thought. I'm gonna be killed by some old Mexican with a sword.

The gentleman positioned himself above Ned and swung the sword, and the next moment Ned felt the blade slicing through his neck.

The soldiers who had been guarding the mansion heard the explosion, and some of those who had been stationed by the entrance left their posts to see what was happening. They ran around to the rear of the mansion, but the officer in charge saw them, and sent them back again. The officer wasn't a fool. The explosion could be just what it looked like: an attack on the cannery. But he also knew it could be a diversion, intended to draw his soldiers away. So, leaving only a few guards at the rear, he led the rest around to the front.

When he got there he saw what appeared to be revolutionaries on horseback, caught in the middle of the wide expanse of lawn, being fired on from two sides: from the house and from the trees bordering the property.

The riders in the middle of the lawn didn't last long after that. A couple of them tried to make a run for it, but it wasn't more than a minute before the whole lot of them were lying dead on the grass.

One of his men told him there were Yaquis inside, so he dismounted and ran in, almost being knocked flat by an riderless horse, slipping and stumbling its way out of the main entrance.

There was a crowd of people gathered around a body. An elderly gentleman was holding a sword, and the officer saw a pool of blood spreading out across the marble floor: the body had been decapitated.

'I have killed one of the Yaquis!' said the elderly genteman.

The officer peered down at the severed head, and saw that beneath the smeared-on greasepaint, the skin was white.

The dead man wasn't a Yaquis. He wasn't Mexican at all: he was an American.

When Lee told Ned that the rest of the gang hadn't followed them into the mansion, he could see the fear in Ned's eyes. So when Ned aimed his horse towards the entrance hall, Lee followed him, knowing how this was going to end. Close by, yet another of the guests produced a small-calibre pistol from inside his jacket and shot one of the gang in the head.

But when Ned's horse fell and Lee heard the crack of bone, he knew right away that Ned wasn't going anywhere.

Lee reached the door, but when he looked outside he saw the rest of the gang in the middle of the lawn being slaughtered. Soldiers were firing at them from the house, while others were firing at them from the trees.

144

He couldn't stay in the house and he couldn't leave. If he charged out there, it would only be a matter of seconds before he was gunned down.

Lee dismounted and ran back into the entrance hall. He still had his rifle, and his revolver. Out of the corner of his eye he saw the gentleman grab a sword off the wall. Lee spotted a doorway to one side of the staircase. He ran to it, wrenched it open and charged down the corridor beyond.

He burst through the door at the end of the corridor into a small room where a man in servant's livery was hiding, smoking a cigarette. He hadn't a chance to do more than gape in surprise before Lee smashed him in the jaw with the butt of his rifle, knocking him out.

Lee slammed the door shut, tore off his Yaquis outfit and put on the servant's clothes. Hearing movement in the corridor, he pumped a few bullets through the door and threw the rifle away.

There was another door. He opened it; another corridor. He ran down it, turned a corner, found yet another door. . . .

And emerged into the night.

A crowd of people – servants and guards – were staring at a building that was in flames several hundred yards away, burning so fiercely he could feel the heat on his face.

Nobody gave Lee a second glance as, dressed in stolen servant's livery, he stumbled off into the shadows.

From behind the trees, Tom Jericho and Dan Harbin saw that the intended massacre had failed. No doubt those members of the gang who had managed to reach the mansion had done *some* killing, but it wasn't the slaughter Walt Crane had intended. It couldn't have been, not with a sizeable part of the gang now dead in the middle of the lawn.

'Was that what we was supposed to do?' asked Dan. 'Prevent a massacre?'

'I guess so,' said Jericho.

'Shame we couldn't have stopped it altogether.'

'We did what we could. Don't see how anybody could have done more.'

'Yeah,' sighed Dan. Then he said, 'We better get out of here, before those soldiers come over here to find out who was doing the shooting. If they see us dressed as Yaquis. . . .'

'Good thinking,' said Jericho. 'Maybe that head wound didn't do any lasting damage after all!'

They rode around to the front of the *casa*. The gates were locked. Jericho remembered overhearing what Walt had said to Ned Grimes about slipping the key back under the gates, so he dismounted and started hunting around in the dirt.

Dan studied the gates, figuring out their options if they couldn't find the key. The gates were thick wood, and the lock was made of iron. Maybe they could climb it, but they'd have to leave the horses behind, which would leave them stranded.

They could try shooting away the lock, but it looked way too strong for that. If Dan had ever learned how to pick a lock, he'd forgotten how and, as far as he knew, Tom Jericho didn't know either.

The hinges also looked too strong to be shot away.

'You found that key yet?' asked Dan.

'If I had,' said Jericho, still scratching around in the dirt, 'don't you think I'd have said so?'

And then a voice from the shadows to one side of the gate said, 'This what you're looking for?'

A man emerged from the shadows, the key in one hand, a revolver in the other.

It was Walt Crane.

CHAPTER EIGHTEEN

'Where's Lee?' Walt asked. 'Where's Ned and the gang?'

Dan Harbin said, 'Something's gone wrong, Walt. They were ready for us.'

'Is my brother dead?'

Dan said, 'We don't rightly know, Walt.'

'Looks like you two got away just fine,' said Walt. 'Explain to me how come you two ain't dead.'

'We gotta get out of here,' Jericho told him. 'The soldiers will be here in a minute—'

'I don't give a damn about no soldiers,' Walt told them. 'All I give a damn about is my brother. Besides, when the soldiers get here, they'll see an honest Mexican holding a couple of revolutionaries prisoner till they arrive.'

Jericho and Harbin looked at each other. They were carrying rifles and wearing bandoleers hung around their shoulders, and gunbelts, and they had spurs on their boots, and horses. Walt didn't have any of that. He was carrying a gun, but he'd dispensed with his gunbelt, and he'd taken off his spurs. With his naturally dark colouring, he looked just like any Mexican peasant who might have happened to pick a gun up from somewhere. A little tall for the average Mexican maybe, but there are taller than average Mexicans, the same as taller than average anything else.

'Tell me what happened,' he said. 'And it had better be good. There's still a slim chance I might let you two live longer than another five minutes.'

After Lee Crane escaped dressed as a servant, he found his way to the stables and stole a horse. Nobody stopped him when he rode out through the gates. The guards were concerned more about people coming in, than people going out.

Five minutes later he was outside the old *casa*. He could hear voices coming from the courtyard. One of them sounded like Walt.

Jericho was saying to Walt, 'Whoever hired you to do this must have set you up,' when there was a knocking from the other side of the gates.

'Hey, Walt! It's me! Let me in!'

It was Lee's voice.

Keeping the gun trained on Jericho and Dan Harbin, Walt unlocked the gates.

Lee slipped through the gap, dressed in some kind of servant's outfit, saw that his brother was pointing a gun at two men he'd thought of as friends, and said, 'What's happening, Walt?'

'That's just what I was asking these two gentlemen to explain.'

Lee said, 'Where're the others?'

'Dead, they tell me,' said Walt. 'I thought you was dead, too.'

'I was lucky. The others in the house, they're dead. Ned, too, by now, I reckon. But most of the gang didn't even make it inside.'

'They were ambushed?' Walt asked.

'I don't know about that,' said Lee. 'But when I looked out, I saw they were being fired on from two sides – from the house and from the trees over here. I saw flashes from two rifles.'

'That a fact?' said Walt, cocking the hammer on his pistol.

Lee was looking disbelievingly at Jericho and at Dan Harbin. 'You betrayed us? Why?'

'Didn't I tell you never to trust nobody but family?' asked Walt.

Lee's shoulders slumped, and for a moment he looked pitiful, almost as if he was going to cry. Then the piteousness was swept away by meanness and he said, '*I* wanna kill 'em, Walt. Let *me* kill 'em!'

But by now Jericho could hear noises behind him. From the other side of the broken-down *casa* he could hear Mexican soldiers breaking through the trees. He couldn't see them, but he knew who they were. Walt heard them too. It would take them all of about thirty seconds to make their way to the front gates.

Walt told Lee, 'We ain't got time!' and aimed the gun at Jericho's head.

Lee's face was red with fury. A thick vein was standing proud on his forehead like a worm under the skin, trying to burst out. '*I said, "I wanna kill 'em"!*' he yelled, his voice shrill.

Lee had taken off his own gunbelt, his gun with it, when he'd been pretending to be a servant, which meant he no longer had a gun of his own.

He lunged at Walt, making a grab for his Colt, at the exact moment Walt fired. The bullet zinged past Jericho's head and crashed through one of the *casa*'s few remaining windowpanes.

'Let go, you dumb son of a—' shouted Walt.

'Give it me!' screamed Lee, insane with rage.

Simultaneously Jericho and Dan Harbin drew their guns and fired. Both bullets hit Walt between the eyes at the same instant, the .45 calibre slugs going right through his skull and slamming into the gates behind.

'Walt!' screamed Lee. He had the gun in his hand now and shot at Dan Harbin, but he didn't even think about aiming, he was just shooting wildly. The bullet missed by a mile. He shot again, but by now his eyes were filling with tears and he'd started yelling meaninglessly, not even forming words. Again the shot went wild, this time hitting a Mexican soldier as he came around the side of the *casa*.

A Mexican bullet hissed through the air between Jericho and Dan Harbin and buried itself in the gate a foot from Lee's head.

Dan said, 'Let's get out of here!'

The gates were still open. Dan ran for the gap, Jericho close behind.

As they passed Lee – blind with rage and tears, screaming like a madman – a bullet hit him in the gut.

Lee didn't buckle. He kept yelling, clutching at his stomach with his left hand, while with his right he carried on firing in the direction from which the bullet had come.

By now Dan and Jericho were outside on the road and pulling the gates shut behind them.

A couple more rifle bullets hit the other side of the gate.

'Shame we didn't grab the key,' said Dan.

'You wanna go back and get it?' asked Jericho.

'I guess not.'

Their horses had taken fright as soon as the shooting had started, and were still inside the grounds somewhere. But Lee had left the horse he'd stolen on the road, and it hadn't wandered far.

They threw themselves on to the back of the horse and hightailed it out of there as a volley of bullets slammed into the thick wooden gate, and Lee Crane finally stopped screaming.

FINALE

Once they'd put a few miles between themselves and Hermosilla, and were pretty sure nobody was following them, they stopped and rested a while.

They were in the hills above the city of Magdalena, travelling back along the same route by which they'd arrived.

While the horse they'd been sharing found itself some greenery to eat, Dan said, 'I reckon my memory's about all come back now. I can't be sure, but that's how it seems.'

'That's good,' said Jericho, wishing he could smoke a cigarette, but knowing that wouldn't be wise. The glow would be seen for miles.

'We still don't know who hired Crane and his boys to dress up as revolutionaries and try to kill all them folks,' said Dan. 'And I want to get the man behind it. Otherwise he'll just hire somebody else to do his dirty work.'

Jericho nodded. 'But how you gonna find this

fella? You can't ask Walt Crane who it was hired him. Walt's about as dead as a man can get.'

'I have an idea about that,' said Dan.

'I had a notion you might,' said Jericho.

Dan's theory was that maybe the man who'd ordered the massacre didn't know that Walt Crane was dead. Walt had been dressed as a Mexican working man, not as a revolutionary, and after he'd been shot twice between the eyes, there hadn't been much of his face left. But the man would know that Walt's gang hadn't done their job properly. The massacre had failed and, furthermore, because the gang had been killed, and were obviously not Mexicans, the Yaquis couldn't be blamed.

Which meant that the politician would be angry.

Dan figured that if he believed Walt Crane was still alive, he would want revenge.

With Dan and Jericho both riding the same horse – sometimes taking turns to ride, the other walking alongside – they made slow progress back to the hideout. By the time they made it to the top of the last rise and looked down on the hacienda, they could see that the empty stables were ablaze.

'Whoever the man sent to exact his revenge,' Jericho said, 'they were sure quick about it.'

Dan swore. He wiped his sleeve across his forehead. The bandage he'd been wearing had come away, but he didn't seem to need it anymore. There was a scab where the bullet had cut a groove, and – though Jericho didn't pretend to be a doctor – it seemed to him that the wound would heal just fine.

'Looks like we missed 'em,' said Dan.

'Maybe not,' said Jericho.

A horse, riderless but with a saddle on its back, wandered into view from behind the hacienda.

'Where'd he come from?' Dan wondered.

'Maybe somebody tied it up, but didn't do a very good job,' Jericho said. 'Maybe it got free.'

'And maybe that "somebody" is still inside the hacienda.'

'Maybe.'

On foot, they led their horse down the hillside till they were a hundred yards or so from the house, then let it go. They drew their guns and advanced on the white-washed building, careful not to make a noise.

They'd only got about halfway when they heard laughing.

They stopped, listened.

'I figure two men,' whispered Dan.

'And both of 'em drunk,' added Jericho.

Inside, they saw a couple of mean-looking men, each with a bottle of booze, sitting in the main room and telling each other what they'd do with Walt Crane, if and when he turned up.

'I'd tie him to a chair out in the desert, slice his belly open and spread his guts out in the sand, and make him watch as they fried,' said one.

The other one laughed at the thought, and said, 'That's nothing. I'd pull out his tongue. . . .'

Both of them were so drunk they were completely oblivious to Tom Jericho and Dan Harbin standing in the doorway. And it looked as if both had already forgotten about the corpse hanging from its neck in the centre of the room. It was the old Mexican woman, Lopita. They'd strung her up from a beam.

Dan fired a bullet into the floor, and both men jumped to their feet. One of them was so drunk he could barely focus. They started to go for their guns, but Jericho said, 'Don't,' and they changed their minds.

The less drunk of the two grinned stupidly and said, 'Neither of you is Walt Crane. . . . We have a picture. This ain't got nothing to do with you. . . .'

Dan said, 'One of you is gonna tell me who sent you, and I don't care how long it takes.'

The drunker of the two men dived behind a table, tilting it on to its side. While Dan Harbin kept his gun on the other man, Jericho fired at the table, but the table was thick enough to stop his bullets. He fired a couple of times, then the hammer clicked on an empty chamber. He swore.

Meanwhile the drunk poked his head up over the edge of the upturned table and fired. But he discovered that booze and shooting straight don't mix. His bullet flew a clear two feet wide of Jericho's head and hit the wall.

Jericho didn't have time to reload. He let his gun drop from his fingers. In less time than it took the drunk to aim his pistol again, Jericho had reached for his throwing knife, plucked it from the sheath hanging from his belt, and sent it spinning through the air.

It hit the man in his left eye, burying itself all the way to the hilt.

Dan said to the remaining man, 'You decided to talk yet?'

It was two weeks later. The opera house in Hermosilla was hosting a performance of Verdi's *Otello*.

Ferdinand Perez settled his immense twenty-five stone bulk into the specially built chair in his private box, a box reserved only for him, and which he never permitted to be used by anyone else. This was not a difficulty for him: Perez owned the opera house. He preferred to enjoy opera alone. He checked his pocket watch. Only five minutes to go. Secure in the knowledge that two of his personal bodyguards were outside the door, he closed his eyes and thought of the young peasant girl who would be waiting for him in his bedchamber when he got home.

'Good evening, *señor.*'

Perez's eyes snapped open. He was about to call out in alarm, when he felt the muzzle of a pistol against his neck and heard the man say, '*Shhhh.* Don't make any fuss. Nod if you understand.'

Perez nodded.

Dan Harbin said, 'Good. By the way, those guards outside in the corridor are taking a nap, so they can't

157

help you. Now I want to introduce you to a lady here whose husband was killed in that raid you organized on that mansion. . . .'

A strong hand twisted his head a little to one side, and Perez found himself looking into the eyes of a white-haired lady, her frail-seeming body encased in an evening gown of black taffeta. Her eyes were as black as the gown.

'You are a lawman?' Perez asked.

'Yeah,' said Harbin.

'You are Americano?'

'Yeah.'

Perez grinned and said, 'You have no authority here. Besides, you can prove nothing.'

Harbin smiled back. 'I ain't planning on arresting you.'

Perez's grin faded a little. 'But if you are a lawman, you will not kill me. . . .'

'No I won't,' replied Harbin. 'I can't speak for the lady, though.'

Sweat broke out on Perez's forehead. The elderly woman had pulled a thin-bladed knife from the folds of her gown. She took a step towards him. Her body might have been old, but her eyes and her movements were determined. 'You will not be the first man I have killed,' she told him in Spanish. 'The last time was when I was a girl, and a disgusting man like you had used me – treated me like I was his toy. I pushed a knife into his heart, just as I am going to push this knife into yours. It was a lifetime ago, but I have not forgotten how. . . .'

Below, the orchestra began to play, and the strains of the overture began to fill the auditorium.

Perez looked at Harbin. 'But. . . . You are a lawman. . . . You cannot allow this. . . .'

'Like you pointed out,' said Harbin, 'I ain't got no authority here.'

It had taken a while for Jericho to make contact. But finally he'd succeeded, and here he was, being introduced to the leader of the Yaquis revolutionaries, a long, lean man with eyes old beyond his years.

'Please, sit down, Mr Jericho,' the man said. 'You will drink with me?'

'Don't mind if I do,' said Jericho.

The man poured tequila into a couple of glasses and, after they'd drunk it, the man said, 'You are not a Yaquis. You are not even Mexican. Why would an Americano want to join our revolution?'

And Jericho said, 'As a matter of fact, I'm half-Mexican, on my ma's side. But even if I weren't, I'd still want to join you. I've seen what the army does to the Yaquis, and it ain't right. And when I see that something ain't right, I want to do something about it. I guess I'm just made that way.'